THE
MEETING

A NOVEL

Denise Ross

The Meeting is a work of fiction. Names, places, characters, and incidents are products of the author's imagination or are used fictitiously. Any resemblance to actual events, locales, or persons, living or dead, is entirely coincidental.

Cover design by CDF Design and Graphics

ISBN 978-0998805405

This much I thought proper to tell you in relation to yourself, and to the trust I reposed in you.

A letter from Captain Gulliver to his Cousin Sympson

Gulliver's Travels
Jonathan Swift

THE MEETING

Chapter One

Karen Moss stood on her balcony and looked at the Pacific Ocean below.   She had come to Ixtapa, the resort town north of Zihuatanejo, Mexico, because she had always felt safe here and at peace with herself.   It had been a marathon drive from her apartment in Washington, D.C. to get here, four days, practically nonstop. She had imagined the calm that would overtake her when she saw the water. How many times had she seen this ocean in the past and marveled at the beauty and majesty of it.   The overwhelming power of the ocean and the relationship it held with humanity. She often pictured herself walking into the water, joining the sea as one. Impossible of course. Now, as she watched the waves below, she pondered what to do next.   I should have stayed in Washington, she told herself, but too late for that now.   But I can't stay in Mexico any longer. They will soon be searching for me, and my passport will be no good. She left the balcony, picked up her purse, left a tip for the maid, then retrieved her small satchel and headed for the lobby.

She checked out and went to the parking lot and got in her car. Then she drove to the airport where she left the car in the parking lot and went in to the terminal to buy a ticket to San Diego.

∞

Two thousand miles to the north, Serge sat at his desk and opened the file marked "Cancelled". The picture of Karen with those giant eyes stared up at him. Karen, the girl he had competed with in high school. Red hair, blue eyes, freckled cheeks. He was shocked to see her face here. It was her, he told himself, older now, but the same girl who had beat him out for valedictorian of their senior class. The same girl he envied day after day, who lived on the rich side of town, unlike him. During the Christmas holidays, he and his mother would drive through the expensive neighborhood, in the northern part of Kansas City, Missouri, where Karen lived. The houses there were massive, sitting on deep, manicured lawns. There was always a tall Christmas tree in the front window, and he could see the sparkling ornaments and lights on the branches. He just knew, too, as they rode past, that there were countless presents under those trees, expensive sweaters, jewelry, and toys for little brothers and sisters.

The paragraph below the picture described Karen's personal information. Unmarried, 33 years old, born in Kansas City, valedictorian of her high school class, graduate of Stephens College, the private, all-girls school in Columbia, Missouri. There she received her bachelor's degree with a double major in English and Spanish. She then moved to Monterey, California, where she earned a master's degree in English at California State University, Monterey. After completing her thesis, she then took a position at the Monterey Peninsula College teaching English to non-native speakers. Five years ago, she moved to Virginia. where she applied and was accepted with the FBI. After the required training and additional education, she spent two years as an agent assigned to the security detail for the first family. Now, and for the past three years, she worked in surveillance and securities fraud, based out of Washington, D.C.

The last time he saw her was five years ago at their ten year class reunion. They only talked for a few minutes, but he learned that she had just broken up with her boyfriend of five years, and was very bitter. She had left Missouri to be with him, and now since the break-up, was considering moving back east, and had even looked into testing for the FBI. Reading that she studied English and Spanish in college surprised him because she had always been superior in math and science in high school. He assumed that she would, like him, pursue engineering, and possibly join her father's firm in Kansas City. The description went on to say that she was engaged to Brian Malic, 35 years old, graduate of Brown, who worked in the White House as an assistant to Daniel Slobe, the chief of staff for the President.

No one had seen Karen for seven days, and now it was Serge's job to find her and eliminate her. Serge had been a professional assassin for eight years, and he was used to receiving assignments, but this one gripped him like no other had. The dossier before him described his rival and yet his unrequited love from high school. How could he go through with this? None of this made sense. In his mind, Karen should be married now, with two kids, and living in a house down the street from her parents. What kind of trouble was she in that someone wanted her dead?

∞

Zihuatanejo, the small fishing town on the Pacific, 20 minutes by taxi to Ixtapa, the Mexican government's Cancun of the West. Alessandro walked along the beach in front of the old hotels. He was headed for his small dive shop at the end of the pier. There were five people signed up for the dive trip to Ixtapa Island. Luckily, the ocean was calm this morning. Each day during the season he took a group of divers out to see the abundant colorful fish around the island. Maybe today they would see a shark, or a small octopus. He smiled at the thought of the pictures he would take of the divers, holding the octopus, eight tentacles hanging down from their hand.

If the ocean remained calm this afternoon, he would go out again with Manuel and Jose, to search in the waters bordering the beach in front of the Palma Real Hotel. Four days ago, Karen Moss, his old friend and English teacher from Monterey, had appeared at his shack after his morning dive. She looked terrible, thin and disheveled, not at all the Karen he remembered from Monterey where she taught him to speak English.

"Do you ever dive in front of the Palma Real?" she had asked him.

"Usually not," he said. "It makes the people on their beach nervous. They wonder why we are invading their private space. And, besides, the colorful fish are located farther north toward Ixtapa Island."

"Would you dive out there for me?" she asked him.

"Of course," he told her.

He would do anything for Karen. They had been close friends when they both lived in Monterey, and he took night classes from her at the junior college. After class, they often hit the nightclub scene in Monterey. She was not much older than him, but they never developed a romantic relationship. She was in love with another man. Alessandro knew he was no match for this tall, blonde haired, perfectly built lieutenant in the Navy, stationed at the Monterey Language Institute. Karen's best friend from high school, Natalie Hunter, often went out with them also. Natalie showed up in Monterey one summer, between jobs, having just inherited a large sum of money from her grandfather. Natalie spent most of her time surfing and partying.

Alessandro had gone diving there in the waters adjacent to the Palma Real beach yesterday afternoon, but had not found what Karen wanted. She asked him to find a box she had dropped into the ocean out by the buoys set up by the hotel to separate the swimming area from the vast Pacific Ocean. To find the box was not an impossible task, just highly unlikely, but he would look again and again if that is what Karen wanted. She was always special in his life, and even though the lieutenant was history, and she was now engaged to a man in Washington, he still held out a chance of winning her over.

Feeling someone behind him, Alessandro slowed his pace, pulled down his baseball cap, and adjusted his Maui Jims. He kept walking and stopped when someone tapped him on the shoulder.

"Natalie", he exclaimed, as he turned to see the lovely woman with jet black hair pulled back in a severe pony tail. "What the hell are you doing here?"

Natalie Hunter, his old accomplice from Monterey, stood before him. "I'm looking for Karen. The last I heard from her she was coming down here to see you. Did she?"

"Well, nice to see you, too," Alessandro answered.

"I know, I know. Guess it's been a long time. You look good," Natalie replied apologetically.

"I guess a long time, probably four years. You look good also. Karen was here two days ago. It was kind of strange. She just showed up. Not that I minded, but she wasn't really herself. Her hair was dyed blonde, and she was nervous and fidgety."

"Did she stay at your place?"

"No, she was at the Palma Real. She came over here by taxi."

Strange, Natalie thought. Karen never stayed at Palma Real. She liked it in town with the locals.

"Was she alone?"

"When I saw her she was. But I only saw her the once."

"Did she say anything to you? About someone being after her?"

"No, but," and here he hesitated, remembering that Karen told him not to tell anyone that she had been here or mention anything about the metal box. But this was Natalie, her best friend.

"But what?"

Surely Karen wouldn't mind if Natalie knew, but why hadn't she told her herself before now? It has to be okay, he told himself. "She asked me to dive in front of the Palma Real, to find a metal box she dropped out there in the ocean."

"What?"

"A metal box. She was on a kayak and dropped it out in the water. She wants me to find it and bring it up."

"And do what with it?"

"I don't know. She just said to call her when I find it."

"When you find it? How in hell can you find a box in the middle of the Pacific Ocean?"

"It's not the middle of the ocean. The waters aren't too deep there in that bay, and right now the ocean is calm. Besides, the box is shiny metal, according to Karen, with jewels on it."

"Jewels," Natalie shook her head. "This is crazy. I've been calling Karen, and she doesn't answer or return my messages."

"When was the last time you saw her?" Alessandro asked.

"I went to her brother's funeral in Kansas City six months ago."

"That's a long time for you guys," he said.

"We don't see each other like we used to. She's busy with her work, and quite secretive these last two years."

"And you?" he asked. "What have you been doing?"

"Just working here and there." Then changing the subject, "Are you going out diving for the box today?"

"Yes, after my group dive, probably, if the weather does not change."

"Can I come?" she asked.

"Sure," he answered with hesitation, "You don't get seasick, do you?"

"Of course not. Remember, I was a surfer in Monterey. I got used to the waves then. I never liked them, but I got used to the swell. No, I'll be fine. What time?"

"Be down here at 2:00 pm, sharp"

"See you then," she said, turning distractedly to head back to town.

Strange, he thought, as he watched her walk away. Natalie and Karen were so close. But Karen had seemed different. And now Natalie, too. So serious and secretive. He watched her as she went up the beach toward the parking lot. She didn't look back, and soon she was out of sight. Alessandro continued to his shack, still confused by his old friends.

∞

"CANCELLED".   Serge read again the large word in black ink. Karen was to be killed. The folder was from a well-connected client in government. He was to carry out the order. He turned in his chair and looked down at the city below him. He could see Union Station, where trains entered and departed Kansas City, and remembered the train ride their high school senior class had taken to Washington, D.C. The other kids had believed him when he said he would work in Washington someday. Why not? He was the smartest boy in the class, with a full ride to MIT. They knew he could do anything he wanted. What would they say today if they knew his job was high priced assassinations?

Chapter Two

At the Delta counter at the airport, Karen paid cash for a first class ticket to San Diego. She produced the same passport she had used to enter the country two days ago. She knew it was only a matter of time until this identity was discovered, and they would know she was in Mexico. They probably knew that already, though, from her first showing of the passport at the border in Juarez two days ago. She left the Caravan in the parking lot of the airport, with the keys in it. She was hoping someone would steal it, and if Daniel's people had discovered she bought a car in Kansas City, they would certainly be surprised to find it in Mexico being driven by someone other than her.

Karen boarded the plane in the first group, and waited nervously in her seat until the plane left the ground, worried that the Mexican police would board the aircraft at any moment and cart her off. Now, she thought, I need to get a car in San Diego. Hopefully she still had time before her identification was on every secret service website as a person of interest, and one to be detained at all costs.

At the San Diego airport, however, to her relief, she rented a car, using her driver's license and her mother's credit card. Again, she couldn't believe her luck that no one recognized her or tried to detain her in any way. Leaving San

Diego at 5:00 pm, she drove through traffic, then hit Los Angeles at 8:00 p.m. She continued north on Interstate 5, stopping only briefly at a roadside café and gas station outside of Bakersfield to fill the gas tank and get coffee and a sandwich, which she took in the car. For another four hours she drove north until she hit the San Jose area, then she took a labyrinth of freeway interchanges going west until she entered Highway One, the coastal highway, and continued north. After a total driving time of eleven hours, she arrived in the town of Half Moon Bay, situated on the Pacific Ocean. Cruising into town, she spotted a motel with a coffee shop adjacent and pulled into the parking lot in front of the office at 4:00 am.

∞

"Serge, it is Acer. Have you found her?"

Serge stared into the phone and almost hung it up. "No, Acer, I", he said with emphasis on the I, "have not found her. Have you found her? You are the one with all the connections. What do you know?"

"We know little. She left one week ago, apparently in her car, and no one has heard from her since. She must be using cash, because her name is not showing on the credit card base. We've contacted everyone she knew, her friends, her family, her fiancé. No one has heard from her, or so they say."

"Fiance?" Serge asked. "What's his name?"

"Brian Malic." Acer answered. "An assistant to the chief of staff for the President."

"He's well connected then. Does the President know what you are doing?"

"No, we haven't told him anything."

"He knows as much as I do, then. Why is finding her, and getting rid of her, so important?"

"I don't even know myself. All I can say is that these instructions come from someone who is very well connected. So don't trouble yourself with the cast list. Just do your job and keep quiet."

Annoyed, but still curious, Serge said, "Maybe she got money from her father. The old man is loaded."

"We checked his accounts, and unless he had cash in the mattress, he didn't give any to her."

"Now what?" Serge asked. "This could be a wild goose chase."

"We'll find her," Acer assured him. "She has to make a call sometime, or contact a friend, and we will know. Just be ready when we need you."

"Don't worry about me," Serge told him. "I will do my job." He didn't tell Acer, however, that he had sent one of his people to Mexico to see if Karen had disappeared south of the border. He wasn't sharing all of his secrets with the malevolent prick.

"We've sent some agents to the West Coast. We know she loves the ocean there. Do you have any other information that would help us? You went to high school with her, right?"

"We graduated in the same year. We weren't friends. We just shared classes together because we were both smart. Taking college prep."

"But she was valedictorian, right?"

"Right," Serge answered, as the hairs stood up on the back of his neck. "Our grades were very similar. They picked her because she didn't have a name like Serge Pachenko." He pulled on his ear, like he did when he felt uncomfortable. "And her parents had money. Mine were poor. Call me when you have her exact location. I have a jet waiting."

Chapter Three

Alessandro finished with his dive group, and he and Manuel put the tanks and gear away in the shop. It was noon, and they walked to the beach side restaurant for lunch.

"Cerveza?" Jorge asked Alessandro from behind the bar.

"No, just a coke. I'm going back out at 2:00 pm."

"Another group?"

"No. Just Manuel, Jose, and I, and a friend from the States. We'll order lunch now also."

Jorge put the cokes on the bar and handed them each a menu. After lunch at 12:45, Alessandro and Manuel returned to the dive shop and prepared for their 2:00 pm trip. Manuel drove the boat to the dock in Zihuatanejo for gas, and Alessandro filled the tanks and checked the equipment. He wondered if Natalie would dive. He had not asked her if she was certified, but if she was, it had happened after they all left Monterey.

At 1:30 Natalie arrived at the shack. She had changed into a black one-piece swimsuit and shorts. Seeing the pricey Oakley's she was wearing, Alessandro said, "You might want to leave the Oakley's here. I've lost too many expensive sunglasses to the water. One burst of wind or big wave and off they go."

She frowned, and he continued, "I've got cheap ones here that I sell to the tourists. Here, I'll give you a pair," and he reached into a cabinet and took out a pair of plain black sunglasses.

"Thanks," she said and put them on in place of the Oakley's, which she handed to him, and he placed them behind the counter.

"Do you want to dive?" he asked her

"No, I don't dive. I'm full of Dramamine now, hoping I don't get seasick."

"You were a surfer. You said you'd be okay," he admonished her.

"And I will. Don't worry."

"Okay," he said, thinking that this could be a disaster. But, the ocean was calm, and the waters in front of Palma Real should be like glass. He was still uncomfortable talking to Natalie abut Karen's request, so to avoid any more questions, he left for the boat as soon as Manuel drove up. Another diver had joined Manuel in the boat. Jose would dive with Alessandro this afternoon.

"I'll be right back", he said, and waded into the water. "I am going to check out the boat."

"Okay," Natalie said and pulled out her large straw hat from her bag. The sun was extremely bright, and it was scorching hot. Natalie pulled the hat down on her head, and dreaded the coming ride in a small boat on the Pacific Ocean. It had been years since she surfed, and she had forgotten how rough the waters could be. 'If he pulls up the box', she told herself, 'it will be worth it.'

Alessandro returned and gathered his gear into a large fish net duffle. Lifting the tank, he said to Natalie, "Ready?"

"Yep. Let's do it."

It took only ten minutes to drive from the small bay at Zihuatanejo around the rocks and cliffs to the private waters in front of the Palma Real. Manuel maneuvered the boat near the buoys set up by the hotel to mark the area for swimming, killed the motor, and dropped the anchor. Alessandro and Jose put on their equipment and tanks. Manuel dropped the flag in the water indicating that there were divers in the water. Then, Jose and Alessandro sat on the edge of the boat and fell backwards into the ocean. Natalie watched as they descended into the clear depths. Soon, though, she could not see them.

"Have you been out here before?" she asked Manuel.

"Dos veces, two times," he answered.

"And found nothing?"

"Nada."

The boat was rocking a bit in the waves, but Natalie's stomach was holding its own. Manuel watched the water where the divers had gone in. Fifteen minutes passed, and a small boat with two men in it approached them from the beach in front of the Palma Real. One of the men yelled to Manuel, "There is no diving here. You need to leave."

"One of our customers lost a bracelet here", Manuel explained, "and we are trying to find it."

"Impossible to find," the man said to him, and studied Natalie, thinking the diamonds were hers.

"We need to try. They are diamonds."

"Diamonds?"

"Yes, very expensive. We will just look this once, and then be gone."

Great, thought Natalie, listening intently. Now hundreds of people will be out here in boats diving for a diamond bracelet that doesn't exist. Satisfied, the driver turned the boat and headed back to the beach.

"Adios," Manuel yelled to the backs of the men, but they did not answer.

"That was a bad idea to tell him that," Natalie said to Manuel. "Now everyone in town will be out here diving. Someone might find the box."

But before Manuel could answer, Alessandro splashed to the surface of the water and held up a metal box with a jeweled lid. Jose was just behind him.

"Wow," Natalie exclaimed.

The jewels sparkled in the bright sun. She reached over the side of the boat and took the box from Alessandro. He removed his mask and air piece and handed them to Manuel. Natalie stared at the box. It was about 10" by 10" by 4" deep. The lid was covered with rhinestones and other multi-colored jewels. She thought they were rhinestones.

"Maybe you weren't so far off," she said to Manuel as she touched the stones. Karen would never have thrown real jewels into the ocean, would she?

Alessandro and Jose climbed the ladder into the boat and removed the tanks from their backs. They both sat down and Alessandro took the box from Natalie's hands.

"So, this is it," he said. "I would never have found it, except the stones were catching just enough light that I saw part of the lid in the sand. If these were rubies, I never would have found it."

"Why's that?" she asked him.

"Red is the first color to go under water. All the colors disappear the deeper you go. I just got lucky with the light hitting the stones just right."

"Now what?" asked Natalie.

"I take the box to my place and call Karen."

"Aren't we going to open it?"

"No. She said not to."

"She hasn't answered any of my calls. How can you be sure you will get in touch with her?"

"She has a new cell number that she gave me."

Again he felt it strange that Natalie did not have the new number. He would share no more information with her. He walked to the back of the boat where he placed the box in a small cupboard with a latch. Natalie watched him carefully.

"Vamos," he said to Manuel and started to pull up the anchor.

Manuel retrieved the red dive flag, and started the engine. As the boat started to glide, Natalie eyed the cabinet, then moved under the awning of the boat, out of the sun. No one spoke on the ride back.

∞

In her motel room in Half Moon Bay, Karen washed her face and collapsed on the bed. Four hours later, she woke and wondered for an instant where she was. Then she remembered, everything. She got up, combed her hair, brushed her teeth, grabbed her purse, and left her room heading for the restaurant to get coffee. As she was going, she noticed two men in dark suits get out of a black sedan and walk toward the office. "Shit," she said. "Christ." She turned immediately and ran back to her room, unlocked the door, stepped in, and let out a huge sigh. Then she thought, maybe they weren't looking for me. Maybe they went in the bar, not the office. But that couldn't be, could it. It was 8:30 in the morning. No, she told herself, these guys had to be feds, that car, those suits. I've been found out.

Unbeknownst to Karen, there was a sign on the office door which read, "Out to doctor's appointment. Back in one hour." The agents had read the sign and gone into the bar to ask about Karen and show her picture to the bartender. The bartender had not seen her. The two men then went into the restaurant where they also showed the picture of Karen to the waitress and the cook. Neither had seen her. They decided to wait for the office to open at 9:30. They sat at a table by a window facing the water and ordered coffee. Here they watched the waves rolling in and out and were oblivious to the action in the parking lot.

Safe in her room, Karen mulled the possibilities. The men would show her picture to the attendant, and he would recognize her from earlier in the morning. Then they would be over here in a heartbeat. But surely, the man she dealt with was on the night shift and had probably been replaced by another person this morning. She had paid cash for the room and used a phony name, so the only way to trace her was to show her picture. Still, she couldn't be sure it wasn't the same man at the desk right now. They could be on their way to her room right now. There was no back door, but there was a window out of the bathroom. She could climb out, run to her car and drive away, hoping that the men would not see her. Or, she could stay locked up in her room until they left, if they

left.   There was no way she could stay.   She
had to get out now.

She quickly gathered her things and threw them
in the satchel, then went to the bathroom,
opened the window, which thankfully was not
jammed, dropped her bag, then climbed out and
jumped to the ground. She ran to the end of the
building and peered into the parking lot.   The
black car was still there.   Maybe, if she was
quick, she could get out of there unseen.   She
stepped from behind the building and ran to her
car.   Carefully, she opened the door, got in and
put the key in the ignition, starting the engine.
"This is it," she thought.   'Either I get away
unseen, or not'.   Putting the car in reverse, she
looked in the rear view mirror.   No movement
from the entrance to the office or restaurant.
"Almost there," she said to herself.   She put the
car in drive and eased out of the parking lot on to
the Coast Highway.   North or south, she thought.
"North," she had an idea where to go.

∞

Father Bruce Manning sat at his desk reading
the draft for the monthly newsletter for the
Pacific Retreat House.   He enjoyed his job as
director of the retreat and had been at it for three
years.   As director, he was responsible for
writing and editing the newsletter each month.
Everything looked fine, and he initialed each
page.   He stood and picked up the draft and

walked from his office to Marge Kennedy's desk where he placed it on top of her in basket. In the morning she would take it to the printer. She had taken today off to care for her grandson. As he stood there, he saw a red Mustang pull into a parking space in front of his office. A blonde woman got out of the car and started walking toward the entrance to the building. She looked familiar, but he couldn't place her. Then he heard the bell. Marge locked the door when she left at 5:00, and he had forgotten to unlock it this morning. He went to the door and opened it, expecting to see a stranger. Instead, he saw Karen Moss.

"Karen," he exclaimed. "Is it really you?"

"In the flesh," she said. "Long time, huh?"

"I'll say. Years. What, four?"

"At least."

"Come in, come in," he told her and pulled the door open wide. She stepped inside, and he motioned for her to follow him into his office. "Sit down, please. You look so tired."

Karen collapsed on an aged leather couch. "If you only knew."

Bruce looked at her wisely, and said, "Why don't you tell me?"

"I will. Right now I really need a drink."

He stepped behind his desk and opened a cabinet and took out a bottle of Jack Daniels. "Jack and coke, right?"

"You remembered," she said.

"I'll never forget that."

Karen smiled. They had met when Karen was working in Monterey teaching English, before she left for the FBI. Bruce was the pastor of the mission church she attended. He brought in many of her students, mostly Mexican immigrants needing to learn English. She and Bruce became close friends.

"You were the cutest priest I had ever seen. What a waste. I know I always said that, but it's true. And look at you now, older, but distinguished. Still handsome."

"Stop," he told her. "And you, a blonde now?"

"That's part of the story," she answered.

He retrieved some ice from a small refrigerator in the corner of the room and filled two glasses. Then he added the whiskey.

"Any coke?" she asked him.

"In the kitchen across the yard, but let's just stick to bourbon right now."

"Fine with me. Leave the bottle out."

Three drinks and two hours later, Karen told him the story of her past year In the FBI, and the secret she had learned when she had been assigned to the White House. Bruce listened quietly as was his habit.

"Does the President know?" he asked her when she had finished with the story.

"I don't think so. They try to keep him pretty much in the dark about everything."

"Who's they?" he questioned her.

"The group of advisers closest to him, especially, Daniel Slobe, his chief of staff. They treat him like he was made of glass or something. To me, it always seemed like someone was pulling the strings. I mean, Hamilton sounds good. He's a great speaker, but in reality, he's scripted. I don't know everything. I only know that my fiancé told me to stay out of his way, and never to initiate a conversation. Like I told you, Brian was included in most of what Daniel learned from the President."

"Have you spoken to Brian?"

"Not since the morning I left Washington. He kissed me goodbye when he went to work. I left that evening. I haven't called him since."

"And Natalie, have you spoken to her?"

"No, we don't keep in touch like we used to. I saw her at Paul's funeral. She was close to my brother, too. That was the last time. I'm afraid to talk to anyone. I don't know who to trust."

"You told me."

"I know," she admitted. "I trust you."

Bruce came around from his desk, took her glass and said, "Let's go into the kitchen and find something for lunch. We missed the meal with the brothers, but we can fend for ourselves. Then I will show you to one of the rooms, and you can get some sleep and take a shower. You are safe here. I have no connections with the government."

"Thanks, Bruce," she said and took his arm.

They walked across the stone courtyard to the dining room for the retreat and then into the kitchen. There were two women in the kitchen cleaning up from the earlier meal.

"Claudia and Marcia," Bruce spoke to them, "this is my friend Monica. She will be staying with us tonight. Will one of you open room 212 for her. And we will just fix ourselves something to eat. Thanks."

The ladies nodded and left the kitchen.

"Do you do this often?" Karen asked. "They left on cue."

"Sometimes," he answered. "People show up at all hours. They're used to it."

"And, I became Monica, nice."

"Well, they don't need to get involved."

After they had eaten roast beef sandwiches and melon, Bruce showed Karen to a room on the second floor of the main building. It was a simple space with a bed, a table and a lamp.

"The bathroom is down the hall," he told her. "You're the only one here this afternoon. We have a big retreat coming on Friday, but today, the floor is all yours."

They entered the room, and Karen set her purse and satchel on the bed. "Thank you," she said and kissed him on the cheek. "You are a life saver."

"Get some sleep," he told her. "I'll see you later."

As he closed the door, Karen laid down on top of the bed. She was asleep soon after her head hit the pillow. Father Bruce walked back to his office, his mind spinning. He wondered if he should call someone.

Chapter Four

Charles Hamilton III stepped from the shower, took a thick white towel from the rod, and began to dry. He wrapped the towel around his waist and walked into the bedroom where his wife sat in bed holding a cup of coffee and surrounded by at least six newspapers. She was reading the San Francisco Examiner.

"Good morning, Sarah," he said to her and walked over and gave her a kiss on the cheek. "I see Emmy came with your coffee and newspapers."

"Yes, just a few minutes ago." She smiled at him. "You were longer than usual in the shower."

"The hot water just felt so good on my back."

"Is the chiropractor coming today?" she asked him.

"No. It's not helping. I'm going to try swimming instead. I'll go to the pool later and do some laps." Ever since he played football in college, his back had bothered him.

"I'm reading that they are preparing for your visit to San Francisco tomorrow. There's an article in here with your schedule. I learn more from the papers than I do from you."

"Sarah," he said, annoyed, "my schedule is planned for the next year in advance. It's available if you want to look at it. Or, just ask Daniel, he knows more about what I'm doing than I do."

She frowned at this, and took a sip of coffee. "Is Daniel going with you?"

"No, not this trip. He's staying here to work on the legislation regarding gun control."

"I thought you had the legislation written already."

"We did, but now it seems like neither side likes the wording."

"Who's complaining the loudest?"

"It's complicated," he sighed.

"And," she encouraged him to go on.

"Well, it's not all it seems on the surface. There are lobbies on both sides. If we show we are pushing for the legislation to limit gun sales, we make the pacifists happy. At the same time, we rally the gun owners and the NRA to fight against the legislation."

"Why don't you just say what you think, and that's that."

"Daniel and one of his assistants are meeting with both sides this week. Daniel with the NRA lobby and Brian with the other side. I just don't want to go into it any further. You know what politics is like. Like I said, it's complicated."

"Charles," she raised her voice, "I'm not ignorant. I've been in politics as long as you. You are playing one side against the other, or you are supporting this legislation for show, and telling the people at the NRA that very detail. There is nothing they like better than a fight about gun ownership. Everyone in the country who owns a rifle or a pistol will be writing and calling their congressmen, and you. The legislation will never pass."

Ignoring her description, and not wanting to discuss it any further, he started walking towards his dressing room. He looked back and said, "Pour me a cup of coffee, would you?"

"Bastard," she said under her breath. She hated being treated like she didn't matter. Then she got up and went into her bathroom. "Pour your own damn coffee," she said outloud, but he didn't hear her.

She closed the door and started a bath. She hated these mornings when she and Charles argued. Not that this was one of their worst disagreements, but it could have been if he had stayed in the room.

She studied her face in the mirror and wondered when their lives had changed. They were still married, still in politics together, and this should be the happiest time of their lives. They had achieved everything they had worked for. He was the President, and she the First Lady. But, every day they grew further and further apart. She worked just as hard as he did, always on display, her clothes, her hair, her children. She didn't know what she wanted anymore, peace and quiet, or just to get back at Charles. She ran her fingers through the gray streaks starting in her dark hair, and sighed.

Walking back to the bedroom, she retrieved her coffee cup and refilled it. Charles had not come out of the dressing room yet. Taking the cup back to the bathroom, she set her cup down on the counter, reached under the sink and lifted out a small bottle of brandy. She twisted off the cap and poured some into her coffee.
She closed the door and locked it, then took off her robe and stepped into the tub. The water was still running, and it was hot, just the way she liked it. She sat down in the bath and cupped the coffee in her hands, taking a sip.

Charles knocked on the door, and said, "I'm leaving now. I'll see you at 10:00 am before I leave."

"I'll be there," she answered through the door.

It was routine for Charles to meet with his wife and two children in the den of the family residence to have a personal moment together whenever he left Washington without them. Charles and Sarah had agreed on this plan when he was elected President. They knew that each time he left, there was a chance he might not come back. And they wanted the children to always say goodbye and get a special hug and kiss from their father. It wasn't that they were morbid, just practical.

Since it was summer, Sarah would not need to worry about their school schedules. She reached over and picked up the house phone and dialed her son's room. C.J. as they called him, answered after three rings.

"Hello, Mom," he said.

"Not too early, is it?" she asked him.

"No. Just leaving. I have a tennis game."

"Your father is leaving this morning for San Francisco. We are meeting at 10:00 am for a brief goodbye."

"Okay, I'll be there."

"Thanks, C.J."

"Love ya, Mom."

"I love you, too," she said.

Smiling, she dialed Carrie's room next. Naturally, Carrie didn't answer, so Sarah left a message on her voice mail. She still didn't like voice mail on this intercom system, but sometimes it was the only way she could communicate with her fifteen year old daughter.

"Carrie, wherever you are, we are meeting at 10:00 this morning to see your father off. He is leaving for San Francisco for a couple of days. Please be there. And call me back so I know you got the message. I'll also call your cell."

She left the same message on her daughter's cell phone. Then, finishing the last of the brandy and coffee, she put the cup on the edge of the tub and sank into the now deep water. She felt a glow from the brandy. Maybe today wouldn't be as bad as she expected.

∞

After Charles left the bedroom, he walked directly to the stairs and down to his office. As he entered the room, he found Madeline, his secretary, placing the carafe of coffee on his desk.

"Ah, thank you, Maddy," he said. "I need it."

"You're welcome, Mr. President," she said. "How was your night? Did you sleep well?"

"All right," he answered. "My back is a little tender. Would you ask Chef to send up granola with berries and yogurt?"

"Certainly. Right on it."

"Thanks. And please call Daniel and ask him to come see me. And tell him to bring Brian."

"Okay," she said and walked to her desk through the side door of the office.

For about half an hour Charles sat at his desk going through the papers left there last night, eating the granola mixed with raspberries and vanilla yogurt, and drinking coffee. At 7:30, Daniel arrived with Brian. Walking in with them, however, was Howard Siefkin, an assistant director with the FBI.

"Good morning, gentlemen. Mr. Seifkin, not a pleasant surprise. Daniel, I need to chat with you and Brian alone."

Siefkin, not the least bit bothered by the unwelcome, said, "Sorry, Mr. President, but I barged my way in this morning. Director Samuels instructed me to come immediately. It is a matter of extreme urgency. He said he would call you."

"I received no call from Samuels," he answered heatedly. "You just don't barge, as you say, into my office without an appointment. This will have to wait until I return from San Francisco."

"I'm sorry, sir. It can't wait," Siefkin explained, looking over at Daniel and Brian. "I'm instructed to speak to you alone."

Charles considered calling the Director, but he knew it would be easier if he just gave Siefkin a few minutes.

"Daniel, Brian, please wait in the outer office. I'll give him some time."

Daniel and Brian left the office and walked to the sitting room beyond. Daniel called the kitchen immediately and ordered rolls and coffee.

"We may as well stay here," he told Brian. "I don't think it will take long with Siefkin. We can have breakfast while we wait."

He sat down in an overstuffed yellow chair, and Brian started pacing in front of the windows which looked out on the lawn. "What is wrong with you? Just sit down and relax."

"I can't relax. I'm so worried about Karen I don't know what to do. I don't think I can stay here any longer. I need to go and find her. I need to be doing something, besides just waiting here and worrying."

"Still no word from her?" Daniel asked him.

"No. Nothing. She left five days ago, and I haven't heard anything. I just feel so helpless. God, I wish she would call."

"And, you talked to her before she left? Friday night, wasn't it?"

"I spoke to her on Friday morning. I left her apartment for work about 7:00 am. That's the last time I saw her. I told her I would see her on Saturday morning. We were going to Tiffany's in Manhattan. We're getting engaged. We had plans to pick out a ring. I just don't understand it. I called her Friday night, late, after we finished working. No answer. I figured she was just out. Then I called her again on Saturday morning to tell her I was on my way over. No answer then either. When I got to her apartment, she wasn't there. I let myself in and walked the whole place. No sign of foul play. She was just gone."

"So you don't know when she left. It could have been anytime on Friday."

"No. She went to work Friday. I spoke to her boss, and he told me she was in all day. She left a bit early, saying she needed to get home and pack for the weekend."

The rolls and coffee arrived, and Daniel instructed Brian to sit down and drink some coffee. As he poured coffee for Brian, he pondered the disappearance of Karen Moss.

"Did Karen work with a man named Saul Abrahms?"

"Yes, for the last two years at the Bureau. He retired six months ago. He was an expert in surveillance and a former agent with the CIA. Why do you ask?"

"He's gone missing, too. Maybe it's related."

Brian thought about this for a moment, but before he could respond, the door from the President's office opened, and Howard Siefkin walked out swiftly.

"He's all yours," he said to the two men as he went by.

Immediately, Daniel walked through the open door and Brian followed behind, his mind still spinning.

"Is it bad?" Daniel asked the President .

"I don't think so," Charles answered, studying his notes. "Director Samuels worries a lot, but he's a good man. I'll look into it on the plane. Right now we need to get on the same base for this gun control issue."

What he didn't tell them was that the director was also concerned about the disappearance of Saul Abrahms. It seems that there was talk of a taped recording he had with him when he went missing. The source had told Samuels that the information on this alleged tape was potentially damaging to the President. They did not have any other information as to where the tape came from or who recorded it, but they were investigating further.

He took the paper on which he had made the notes about the tape and dropped it into his briefcase, which sat open on the floor by his chair. Daniel stared at the paper. He was annoyed he had not been included in the briefing, and now he was truly worried about the whereabouts of Saul Abrahms. He wanted to grab the notes from the floor and grill the President, but he refrained, knowing it was useless to pursue it now.

Chapter Five

Natalie hung up the phone and stood to look out her window at the sun setting on the Mexican street below. There were shoppers with packages, kids out of school, and tourists in shorts and sunglasses. She was almost finished with her assignment. One more step and her job would be complete. She regretted right now her profession more so than at any other time since she started working for Serge. It was never meant to involve anyone she actually knew, only strangers would be impacted. I made a decision years ago, she told herself, to divorce my feelings from my work. But could she really kill Alessandro? Surely, it would not come to that. She took her pistol from her purse, and checked the clip for cartridges. She also fitted the silencer to the barrel and then removed it. She put the gun and silencer into her purse and zipped it closed. Then, she left her room and ran down the stairs. With a straw hat covering her black hair pulled back in a ponytail and her white shorts, she looked like an ordinary tourist. She stopped a taxi and ordered a ride to the address which Serge had given her. It took only a few minutes to arrive at Alessandro's apartment. Natalie paid the driver, entered the building and climbed up the three flights to number 320. She knocked on the wooden door and waited. In a moment, Alessandro opened the door.

"Natalie. This is a surprise. How did you know where I live? I thought we were meeting tonight. Isn't that what we said when we got back from the dive?"

Natalie entered the apartment, closed the door behind her, and looked around the sparsely furnished living room. "Yes, we said we would meet tonight, but I needed to come and see you now. I need to get that box from you. I need to take it back to the States."

"How did you find me? I didn't give you my address," he said, while unconsciously glancing toward the back room of his apartment. "What's going on with you anyway? Both you and Karen are acting so strange. I haven't seen either one of you in years, and in three days, I see both of you down here in Mexico."

"I'm on an assignment. Your address was given to me when I reported on the dive. I was hired by someone to find Karen and the box. I missed her, but I did find the box. Now I need you to get it for me. I'm deadly serious, Alessandro. Don't fuck around with me. You just looked toward the back room. Is it there?"

Alessandro looked again toward the back room, then immediately turned his eyes back to Natalie. "It's not here," he told her. "I put in a safe place."

"Right," Natalie responded, as she turned to close and lock the door. She took the gun from her bag, attached the silencer, and pointed it at Alessandro. "Let's just walk to that back room and have a look."

"Jesus Christ, Natalie. What's happening here? Are you really going to shoot me?"

He didn't move, and she waved the gun at him and said, "This isn't a game, and I am really sorry to be doing this to you, but I can't leave here without the box. If I have to shoot you to get it, I will."

Stunned, Alessandro turned slowly and started walking toward the back of the apartment. Natalie followed close behind. Then as he walked through the doorway to his bedroom, he spun around and lunged at Natalie, trying to knock her down. Natalie, however, was too quick for him. She stepped back and tripped him with her foot. Alessandro fell to the floor.
"It's not fucking here! I told you. I left it somewhere safe."

Alessandro rose to his knees and looked up at Natalie. "You're not going to shoot me, Natalie." he said, and as she hesitated, he reached up and knocked the gun from her hand. It slid across the floor, and both of them scrambled to get it. Alessandro threw his body on the gun, but Natalie jumped on him and sliding her hand under his torso, grabbed the gun. Instinctively, her finger rested on the trigger. Alessandro struggled to get up, and Natalie fired the gun. He slumped to the floor, blood pouring from his stomach.

She stood, and without stopping, walked into the bedroom and started searching for the box. She looked under the bed, in the dresser drawers, in the closet and the bathroom. In twenty minutes, she had searched the entire apartment, but no box. Alessandro lay lifeless on the floor. The blood had started to coagulate. Natalie had walked past his body many times. Now, she stood over him, considering what to do next. A feeling of revulsion gripped her, and she thought she was going to faint. But she took a deep breath, then unlocked the door and left the apartment. There was no one in the hallway. Walking slowly down the stairs, she entered the street and pulled a note from her purse. She stopped a taxi and instructed the driver to take her to the address on the paper. It was the home of Manuel.

∞

Karen woke up from her first full night's sleep in seven days. She looked around the room, and it took a minute for her to remember what had happened yesterday. She had collapsed on this bed, and slept until the sunrise. She desperately wanted to call Brian and her parents. But she knew she couldn't. The two men from the motel might be on their way to the retreat at this very moment. The FBI had alerted the agents to the haunts and favorite places of Karen Moss, to her friends, and her family. She, herself, in the past two years, had investigated minute details about others. She knew the data bases they would use, and the means to contact everyone she had ever known. She was certain they had spoken to her parents by now, but she knew her parents would tell them nothing. Especially that her father had given her $80,000 in cash from a safe he kept under his house.

On the Friday night, after Saul left her apartment, Karen had driven almost non-stop to Kansas City. When she reached her home town, she called her father, and he met her with the cash at a downtown car lot. She purchased a used car paying $10,000 cash. The dealer did not ask too many question when she handed him the money. Wasn't cash really king? She said goodbye to her father then drove out of town in the grey Dodge Caravan. Karen's father, at her request, had brought to her the silver box with the jeweled lid from her room. It was a gift from him ten years ago. She placed the tape that Saul had given her in a hidden compartment in the lid. Then she put the box in her bag which she had packed for her trip to Manhattan. She drove south from Missouri into Oklahoma then Texas, crossing the border into Mexico at

Juarez. She carried a passport and I.D. from a prior investigation with the Bureau. The name on them was Sofia Solcedo. No one asked her any questions at the border, except was she traveling for business or pleasure. Pleasure, she said, just a vacation from work. "And, what do you do?" the Mexican agent had asked her. "I am a school teacher," she lied. In Juarez, she found an electronics store and made a copy of the tape, returning the original to the lid of the box. She also purchased a prepaid cell. She destroyed her original cell by placing it under the tire of the car once she crossed the border. On the return to the States, she used the same credentials.

It had been a week since she left home, and she worried that Daniel's people would know that she was traveling under this alias. Since she had seen the two men in Half Moon Bay, she was certain now that Daniel knew she had been in Mexico. His people must be looking up and down the Pacific Coast for her now. He had no doubt enlisted the help of the secret service and the FBI to find her. Being the chief of staff, he wielded the power to start investigations, and to stop them. Karen knew how ruthless Daniel could be. She had seen him in action at the White House. Anyone who crossed him would never get close to the President. There were rumors, which she believed, that he had eliminated, permanently, opponents of Charles Hamilton, dating back to their days in Chicago when Charles was mayor there. Of course, there had been suspicions, but no prosecutions ever resulted from any of Daniel's actions. Someone would just disappear, never to be heard from again. Karen knew who she was running from, and she was scared.

She showered in the bathroom at the end of the hall and dressed again in the khakis and t-shirt she had worn when she arrived. She walked down to the kitchen where she found Bruce and several of the brothers eating breakfast. Bruce immediately got up and guided her to a small table by the window, where they both sat down. A waiter appeared with coffee and juice.

"What do you want for breakfast?" he asked her.

"Anything," she replied gratefully, then added, "just cereal and milk. I need to get on the road."

Bruce looked at her and nodded, then said, "Nothing for me. I've already eaten."

When the waiter left, Bruce said, "You know, you don't really look like yourself. I mean besides the hair and the clothes. I guess It must be the worry on your face."

"I guess that's good, I mean, not looking like myself, but, I just wish I could go back. I think I made a terrible mistake by running. If Saul and I had just stayed in Washington." Then, she added sadly, "Too late for that now."

"What can I do to help you?" Bruce asked her.

"Well, I need a car. I am afraid to keep driving that Mustang. I am sure the two men at the motel got the license number from the manager, so now it is not safe. Do you know where I could buy one cheap?"

"I've got a Ford Taurus that was donated to us last week. It's just sitting in the garage for now. You can take it."

"That's amazing. How much shall I pay you for it?"

"Nothing. Save your money. When all of this is over, we can get it back."

"Thanks, Bruce," she said quietly. "I'll leave the Mustang here. It is a rental, so would you return it for me. The paperwork is in the glove compartment. It might be a good idea to wait a few days, though. You might get pulled over, and not by the local police."

"The Mustang can go in the garage in place of the Taurus. We'll take care of it."

The waiter arrived and placed a tray on the table which held several small boxes of cereal, a bowl, and a pitcher of milk. Karen poured a box of corn flakes into the bowl and added some milk.

As she began to eat, Bruce asked her, "Where is the tape now, Karen?"

"If you don't know that, you will be safe," she told him. Then she pushed back her chair and stood up, "Let's go and get that car. It's time I got on the road."

Bruce stood also, and they walked to the back door of the dining room where he led her to a garage at the back of the property. He pulled open the old wooden door, exposing various makes and models of cars. He entered the building and removed a set of keys from a cabinet on the side wall, then he motioned for Karen to follow him to a tan Ford, where he opened the door and told her to get in. He then gave her the keys and stood back. "Hopefully, this car takes you to safety."

She reached for him and gave him a hug. "Thank you for this. I should be safe in this car. I will look like I work for the government."

"Just get yourself out of this mess," he told her. "And, please call me. Maybe I know someone who can help you."

"I probably won't. I am already sorry I got you involved. I promise after this is all over, I will get in touch."

"Do you know where you are going?"

"I heard last night on the radio in my room that the President is in San Francisco today for a fund raiser. It made me start thinking of a way out of this."

"What are you going to do?"

"First, not tell you. The less you know, the better. Like I said, I have probably put you and the rest of the brothers in jeopardy. I am sorry to be so blunt, but I want all of you to be safe."

"We can take care of ourselves. Don't worry about us. We have God on our side, remember?"

Karen smiled and so did he. She got in the car, and Bruce closed the door. Karen started the ignition and put the car in reverse. Bruce guided her out of the garage, and she stopped once she was outside the building. Karen opened the window and looked up at him.

"Thank you, I…" she stumbled for words.

"It's okay," he said, and touched her on the hand. "Be safe. I will pray for you."

"Goodbye, Father," she said and looked through him. "I don't know when I will see you again."

"Soon, I hope. Under happier circumstances. I do want my Taurus back!"

She smiled at this, put the car in drive and started down the steep drive to the street. She turned south and headed for the freeway which would take her to San Francisco.

Chapter Six

That morning after the President said goodbye to his family and got on a plane for San Francisco, Brian and Daniel met each other at noon and went to lunch at one of their usual restaurants in Georgetown. Daniel ordered his usual Grey Goose martini, and Brian his usual club soda. They studied the menu quietly.

Brian spoke first. "I've hired someone to help me find Karen. Winston Morris. You know him, former CIA. If anyone can find her, he can."

"Morris? I do remember him. Kinda creepy. Every time I saw him, I thought of Dracula. Those eyes."

"That's crazy. He's a good agent."

"Then why did he leave the CIA?"

"I don't know. Maybe the eyes." Brian smiled.

"Nice to see you smile," Daniel said. "Has he learned anything?"

"He is pretty sure she went to see her parents in Kansas City. He spoke to a neighbor who is a friend of Karen's mother, and she told him that Karen had contacted them for help, but didn't say anything else."

"But Morris spoke to her parents directly?"

"Yes. They said they had not heard from her."

"You mean they lied."

"Yes, I guess," Brian stuttered.

"I know this sounds harsh, but, do you think Karen was getting cold feet?"

"No," Brian answered, taken aback. "Karen always spoke her mind. She was happy. She wanted to get married, have kids. It has to be something else."

"Have you talked to the police?"

"Yes. Two days after she was gone, I went down and met with a Lt. Karlsen. He took a missing person's report and asked me all sorts of questions. Like, had we had a quarrel, was she distraught, suicidal? I told him nothing was wrong the last time I spoke to her. We were planning a weekend in Manhattan. I was taking her to Tiffany's to get a ring."

"Have you talked to her father?" Daniel asked.

"Yes, he's heard nothing either. Or so he said. I also talked to her boss at the FBI and some of her friends at work. No one has heard a word.

At least that is what they are saying. Maybe she is on some top secret assignment."
"Was she working on anything top secret?"

"She wouldn't tell me if she was. Her car is gone, and some of her clothes. Everything else is still in her apartment. Do you think Siefkin's visit this morning had anything to do with Karen?"

"I doubt it. But, didn't she work for the first family security detail for a while?"

"She did. Regarding the safety of the children, and watching the First Lady. You know, Sarah's drinking is legendary, hurts the kids the most. Karen spent a lot of time with the older daughter. But that assignment ended years ago, and Karen started working on securities fraud. I mean, I thought she did. I don't know what to believe now."

The waitress appeared with their lunches, and Daniel ordered another martini. He took a few bites of his crab salad, then said, "You know, there is another missing person." Brian looked up from his French fries. "Saul Abrahms. I think he worked with Karen."

"Saul", repeated Brian. "I remember the name. How long has he been missing? Are you saying they are together?"

"No," Daniel said quickly. "Saul is old enough to be Karen's father. I just thought of it, now."

"Who told you he was missing?"

"Bob Poole," Daniel lied. "An agent who belongs to my gym. Said he didn't show up for poker last week, and Bob called his home. His wife said Saul had just disappeared. She did not know where he went. It's been about a week, the same time Karen has been gone."

"You think it's related?"

"I don't know. It just came to me."

"I'll tell Morris. Maybe they are related. Saul Abrahms who works with Karen?"

"I'm not really sure," Daniel lied again. "Just that they are both FBI."

The waitress brought Daniel the second martini, and he drank it as Brian finished his cheeseburger and fries. Daniel's crab salad remained mostly untouched on the plate. "I have an appointment at 2:00 pm," Daniel said as he finished the martini. "He handed Brian $50 for his lunch. I'll talk to you before 5:00."

"Sure," Brian said, looking at him strangely. "Talk to you later."

Strange, he thought. This whole lunch was strange. Dracula? Creepy eyes? Saul Abrahms missing with Karen. I've got to call Morris now. He waved at the waitress and left $100 on the table. As he approached the door he scrolled in his phone for Morris' number. Maybe he would have some good news this call. In his gut, though, he knew Karen was in trouble, and now he knew there was someone else involved.

∞

At 2:00 pm, Daniel sat in his office reading a brief written by a lawyer for the NRA. There was a light knock, a moment, and then Sarah Hamilton entered and walked to a leather chair facing his desk. She sat down and for a few seconds they just looked at each other, saying nothing.

"What happened this morning?" she asked him. "From your message, it sounded like you had some news from Saul."

"I hope not," he said. "This morning as Brian and I were waiting for Charles, this assistant director from the FBI showed up and demanded to see Charles, alone, no appointment. He convinced Charles it was critical, and Brian and I left them alone. He was in there about 30 minutes. When he came out, Brian and I went in, and I asked Charles what it was all about, but he would tell us nothing."

"But you think it was about the tape?" Sarah asked.

"I don't know. I know I'm paranoid. Aren't you?"

"That's not the word. Suicidal. Scared shitless," she said.

"There's more," Daniel added with resignation. "Brian's hired an ex-CIA agent to find Karen. And Brian will tell him that Saul is also gone. It won't be long until he puts things together."

"How do you know who Saul talked to? How do you know there was a copy of the tape? He told me he didn't make a copy, that he gave me the only one."

"And you believed him? Sarah, this is fucking Washington. There's always a copy of the tape. Saul, your trusted friend, made a copy before he gave it to you, believe me. And he probably confided in Karen Moss. Maybe he even gave her the tape."

"Jesus," Sarah groaned and sat back in the chair, "what happened to him? Where's Karen?" She looked hard at Daniel, and saw for the first time in ten years, a stranger. After seven years working with him on political campaigns for her husband, and for the last three years meeting him secretly, making love, sharing intimate details of her life with Charles, she now saw evil. Wicked, she thought, wicked.

"I have been a fool," she finally said. "I thought I loved you. I never loved you. You were just a game, a dangerous game."

"Don't be a bitch, Sarah. Haven't you done enough? If this comes out, we will have nowhere to hide. You have got to find out if Charles knows. And you've got to try and find Saul."

At this, Sarah exploded. She stood up and leaned into the desk, "You call me a bitch! I guess I was good enough for you in bed all these years, spilling my guts, telling you secrets that I knew I shouldn't. But I fell for you, or I thought I did. I guess the booze kept me going, let me think that you really cared for me. You never cared for me. You just wanted to get into my head, to get one up on Charles. It must have been hard for you all these years, being his patsy. Doing everything for him. But, what about Daniel? Hah, without Charles, Daniel is nothing. So you took me. And I was just so easy. God, I could kill myself. No wonder I drink."

"Are you done?" Daniel scorned. "Sit down. Listen to me. We need to find that tape. We need Saul and we need to know if Saul told Karen anything, or worse, gave her a copy of the tape."

Sarah took a deep breath and sat back down in the chair. Daniel continued, more calmly now. "I'm moving ahead as if she has the tape, that Saul for some reason, confided in her. I have people looking for her in two countries. We are looking for Saul also. I'm sorry about what I said, but you brought Saul into this, and I just think you might be able to find him."

"Don't you think I've tried to contact Saul? I've called his cell, called his wife, and nothing. She doesn't know where he is. You know, don't you, that Saul was in the CIA when he was younger. He spent years in Eastern Europe, many of them under cover. He knows how to hide. And, God help me, he knows surveillance." She stopped here for a moment and stood up. "Look, Daniel," she said firmly, "You're the brilliant one, the cagey one, always in the right place at the right time. I will give you one week to find the tape, or Saul, or Karen, whoever. After that I am going to tell Charles everything." She then turned and walked quickly out the door, giving him no chance for reply.

Daniel sat there for a moment, letting this ultimatum sink in. Finally, he picked up the phone, dialed a number, and waited. "Hello," said a voice on the other end after three rings.

"Acer," Daniel said, "there have been some complications."

Chapter Seven

When Saul showed up at Karen's apartment, she had been packing for a weekend in New York with Brian. Her suitcase sat open on a chair, ready for any last minute items she might remember. They were going to Tiffany's to pick out an engagement ring. The one she was wearing had come from her old jewelry box. She loaned it to Brian who gave it to her. Then they made plans to go to Tiffany's in Manhattan to buy the real one. She pictured them walking into the store, speechless and amazed at the glass counters glittering with diamonds. Brian was picking her up in the morning at 10:00 am.

Karen was checking what she had packed when the bell rang to her apartment. She walked to the door and buzzed the intercom. "Who is it?"

"It's Saul Abrahms," the voice answered.

"Saul? The FBI Saul?" she asked.

"The same. I need to talk to you."

"Come on up," she said, and pushed the button to unlatch the street door.

In a few seconds, Saul knocked on the door. Karen peered through the peephole and confirmed it was him. "Come in, Saul," she said as she opened the door, looking him over. "It's been a long time, a year anyway," she told him.

"A little over," he said, "since I retired."

"Come on in," she motioned for him to move into the apartment. "Sit down. Would you like something to drink? Coffee, wine, beer?"

"Coffee," he replied without hesitation.

"Okay," she said. "I'll go put the water on. I hope instant is okay."

"It's fine," he said and nearly collapsed into the flowered overstuffed chair at the edge of the room.

Karen came back from the kitchen and gave him a curious look. "What's going on? I haven't seen you in over a year, and you show up here at 10:00 pm on Friday night looking like something from a national disaster."

"It is a national disaster," he said, "at least for me it is."

Karen and Saul had worked together in the fraud division of the FBI for two years after she completed her detail with the President's family at the Whitehouse. Saul was an expert in communications, wiretapping, recordings, video surveillance. He taught Karen how to use the latest technology to gather information on anyone without their knowledge.

Karen sat down on the couch facing Saul and said, "Tell me what is going on."

He looked at her, then out the window at the car lights in the street below. She watched him in silence. Finally, he began.

"You know I retired a year ago April, and I thought I was going to love having nothing to do. But after a few month I thought I was going to go bonkers. Too much time on my hands. My wife told me to get out of the house, I was driving her crazy. So I started my own consulting business. Consulting is probably not the word, it was more like spying. I've been pretty busy. You'd be shocked at how many people want to spy on other people. Mostly lovers, husbands or wives, suspecting the other one of cheating. Some business people looking to get the scoop on a deal, news writers needing a story. I wasn't choosey, I just went where the money was."

Karen just listened, saying nothing.

"Two weeks ago, I had a call from a woman who wanted to get information on her daughter. That's another area, parents watching their kids. Well, this woman said she needed to know if her daughter was using drugs. She thought she was, but she needed to be sure before she approached the girl. You see, this mother and daughter are quite famous, and any story like this would be a big scandal. Well, I set up a video surveillance unit in the girl's bedroom. The design was easy, only the access was difficult. But with the mother's help, we managed it. I put an SD card in a phony smoke detector which I placed on the ceiling in front of the door going into the hallway. The action would be controlled by the mother. When the daughter was home in her room, the mother would start the recording, and before bed at night, she would turn it off."

"This mother and daughter don't talk?" Karen asked.

"Yes, they talk, but you don't understand. This girl is not going to confess to using drugs. No kid will tell her parents they are using. You've forgotten what it is like to be a teenager."

"I never did drugs. I wouldn't know. But I have recorded drug deals with you. Go on, what did you find on the tapes?"

Just then the tea kettle whistled from the kitchen, and Karen got up to make the coffee. Saul sank back in the chair and stared out the window. Karen returned carrying two mugs of steaming coffee. "Do you take cream or sugar, no black, right?"

"Black, right."

Karen set the mug on a table by the chair and then sat back down on the couch. Saul looked toward the door, and asked her, "You did lock that door, didn't you?"

"Two dead bolts," she answered. "Boy, this must be some mother and daughter."

"I just want to finish the story, and then you'll understand."

"Go on then," Karen said, blowing on her coffee and taking a tiny sip.

"Well, the SD card is a small disc, and to view it the mother would have to insert it into her computer. It had eight hours of run time, so I told the mother after eight hours of recording to remove the SD from the unit and play it in her computer. Trouble was, her computer didn't have an SD player. DVBD's only."

"You didn't know this?"

"She told me she had a MAC. All MACs have SD players. Turns out she had a Dell. Turns out she's not very technical. I bet she hasn't shopped for anything except mascara in the last ten years."

"Who is this person?" Karen asked.

"You'll see. Well after a couple of days, she called me, this time on my secure cell, and told me she could not play the tape. So, we arranged to meet and I would take the SD and copy it to a DVD for her. I'll tell you right now I was as uncomfortable as hell about this. I got the disc, took it back to my shop, and could have copied it without seeing what was on it. After all, this is a teenager, in her bedroom for Christ's sake. But, I couldn't stop myself. Besides, as I rationalized, I needed to make sure it worked. Hell, if there was nothing on it, it would be worthless anyway, and we would have to start over. I played the SD, than made the copy. Trust me, this is the hardest thing I have ever done. Honest to God, I don't know what to do next."

"Saul, did you give her the DVD?"

"Yea, we met last night, and I gave it to her."

"Did you talk at all? Did you give her another SD?"

"Saul sat there and stared again out the window. Dejected, he said, "We spoke only briefly. I gave her another blank SD, then said I was in a hurry, working on a case. For her to get in touch with me later."

"Has she called you?" Karen knew something was dreadfully wrong. "Who is she? Who is this woman and daughter?"

"Do you have a MAC?" Saul asked her.

"I do. It's in here," she said, and started toward her bedroom.

Saul followed, removing the small disc from his inside coat pocket. "Play it," he said, handing the disc to Karen.

Karen took the disc and inserted it into her computer. The tape began, nothing at first, then on the screen, a teenage girl, about fifteen or so, brown hair, cut in a long layered shag. Karen immediately recognized her, and looked at Saul.

"That's right. Carrie Hamilton."

Now Karen had a sinking feeling in her stomach. The tape continued, Carrie sitting on her bed, texting on her cell phone. Then nothing. The tape started again, must be the next day, and Carrie is dressed for tennis. She answers a phone call and leaves the room. But the tape does not stop. There is just a shot of Carrie's bed, unmade, with CD's and books on it. Next a man and woman appear and collapse on the bed. Kissing and touching each other, they proceed to make love on Carrie's bed, not even stopping to remove the books or the CD's.

"Jesus Christ," Karen moans. "This is for real?"

The tape continues to run. The love making is quick, and the few clothes they remove are put back on. The two lovers sit up and kiss one more time, then the man straightens his clothes and leaves the room. The woman falls back on the bed, staring at the ceiling. She touches her breasts and her crotch, then slowly sits up. Then she stands, adjusts her skirt and sweater, steps into her sandals, and leaves the room.

Karen is stunned into silence. Saul does not speak. The tape continues. Carrie returns to her room, but the tape stops, having run out of recording time. Saul and Karen still do not speak. Finally, Karen says, "Sarah Hamilton and Daniel Slobe, lovers? In the White House, on tape? Jesus Christ, is she crazy? Did she do this on purpose?"

"She's not crazy," Saul answered. "She didn't know this was on the tape."

"And you did not tell her?"

"What was I gonna say, I have you and your husband's Chief of Staff, on tape, fucking your brains out?"

"Christ, Saul, how did this happen?"

"Their affair, or the tape?" Not waiting for an answer, he went on. "Sarah drinks. Everyone knows that. She obviously forgot about the tape in one of her stupors. Turned it on in the morning and left it running. Maybe they met in Carrie's room more than this time."

"Oh, Jesus. Has she seen this?"

"I'm guessing she has. She has called me at least ten times. I haven't returned her calls. I don't know what to do. I've been driving around. I found myself on your street, and here I am."

"And, your car? Parked in the front?" she asked him.

"No, I parked in the back. In one of the covered spaces."

Karen walked over and turned off the light beside the bed. The she ejected the tape and walked to the living room. There she closed the blinds and turned on the television.

She turned to Saul, and said, "You have got to go to the airport right now. Don't stop for anything. Don't pack, don't call your wife. Just buy a ticket out of the country. If Daniel has seen this, and Sarah has told him the story, you're dead. I just hope he hasn't alerted the airports."

"Maybe she hasn't shown it to him yet."

"You can hope," Karen said.

Saul looked at his feet, and said, "I'm sorry. I don't know why I came here, but I know you are engaged to Brian, and I guess I just thought you could talk to him, and stop this thing before it destroys everyone."

Karen sat down on the couch and sighed. "Neither one of us is safe now," she said.

"But they don't know about you," Saul told her.

"Don't kid yourself. Daniel knows we worked together and I was assigned to the first family. He will think of me immediately when he learns you supplied the tape and now have disappeared, and won't take a call from Sarah. I'm not going to wait around to see what happens next. Daniel reacts and asks questions later. You remember that apparent suicide four years ago. The congressman who threatened to expose the President in one of his infidelities. I'm sure it was Daniel, or one of his people."

She stood and walked over to the chair where her travel bag sat open. She latched it shut, then she picked it up as well as her purse and went to the front door and opened it.

"You first," she told Saul.

He walked out and Karen followed. She left the television on.

Chapter Eight

In five minutes the taxi had wound through the streets of Zihuatanenjo and climbed up a slight hill to a neighborhood of small stucco homes. The driver stopped at the address Natalie had given him. Natalie opened the door of the taxi, reached into her purse and paid the driver. She walked up a few steps and across a small porch to the wooden front door. Here she knocked and waited. There was no answer. She knocked again. Still no one came to the door. The taxi had returned down the narrow street in the direction of town. Natalie surveyed the area, and seeing no one, she tried the door. It was not locked. She looked around again and then entered the small front room. There were curtains on the open windows facing the street, so she would be seen by anyone passing by.

It was a small house with two bedrooms, the living room, a kitchen, and a small bathroom.

She walked through all the rooms first very quickly, looking for any obvious hiding places for the jeweled box. Then she started in the bedrooms, opening the drawers in the chests and rifling through clothes as fast as she could. She searched in the small closets on the floors and the shelves. Finding nothing, she returned to the living room. She didn't find it here either. Finally, she rummaged through the cabinets in the kitchen and bathroom. Nothing. She went out the back door from the kitchen and ran down the steps onto a patch of lawn. There were no hiding places out here that she could see. So she stepped over a slight fence into an alley and walked to the adjacent street.

Feeling desperate now, knowing that Alessandro was dead, and Manuel was the only other person who might know where the box was, she started walking down the hill towards the town and found a taxi and instructed the driver to the pier at the town beach. Leaving the taxi, she ran down the beach to Alessandro's shop. It was always left open, and she went in and searched every inch of the place for the jeweled box. It was not there. She then walked to the end of the beach and looked at the dive boat anchored off the shore. I have to swim out there, she thought. It might be on the boat. So she removed her clothes down to her underwear and walked into the warm water, and swam the short distance to the boat. The ladder was down, so she climbed easily into the boat. Here she also performed a thorough search, but found nothing. Alessandro told her he had put the box in a safe place, but she had to make sure it wasn't still in the cabinet from this afternoon. The box wasn't on the boat, nor in the dive shack, nor at Alessandro's apartment or Manuel's house. Where had he put it? Why is this box so important anyway, she thought. Why was I hired to kill for this box? She thought back to the phone call she had from Serge. He had said, "Find Karen. Then call me." Natalie had just assumed when Alessandro mentioned the box that it must be important to finding Karen. Or, she thought, if she had the box, she would have some power over Serge. Now, no Karen and no box. I'll just stay here tonight, she thought. Manuel will show up in the morning for the usual dive, and I will question him then. He must know something, she told herself, but deep down in her gut, she knew Manuel would not come back to the dive shack. He was probably on his way out of Zihuatanejo by now. He looked through me, he knows what I've become, she told herself. Alessandro could not see it, but Manuel, he knew.

Staying the night at the hotel on the beach wouldn't be so bad. This way she could call Serge in the late morning and tell him she waited for Manuel, but he never showed up. She was for once regretting the kill. Even though Alessandro's death had been accidental, she knew in her heart that she would have shot him anyway. There was an urge, uncontrollable, that overtook her. Each time. She was addicted to murder. She jumped from the boat and swam back to the shore, put on her clothes, picked up her sandals and returned to the shack to retrieve her bag. No one had been there. The she started walking toward the open bar at the La Sirena Hotel. She sat on a stool, and ordered. "Corona, por favor, con limon."

At 10:30 pm that night the President dove into the heated pool at the Sheraton in San Francisco. The pool was empty except for him. On the concrete decks stood seven secret service agents, all watching him do laps. He thought as he swam and smiled inwardly, so many people to watch an old man swim. Not that he was that old, 49, but he felt centuries older. I can't even remember the last time I swam alone. He thought of Blue Lake, in his home town, where he swam as a boy. I wonder if it is still there. I'll go and see the next time I am in Bloomington, he told himself. Five laps, ten, he still didn't feel tired. In fact, he felt better than he had in days. I've got to keep swimming, he also told himself. After an hour of swimming and periodically looking up at the seven agents, he stopped and got out of the pool.

One of the men in a suit handed him a towel and said, "That was quite a swim, Mr. President."

"Yes, it was, Carl, and I feel terrific. Ready to start a good nights' work, eh?"

Charles dried off and headed for the double glass doors which were being held open for him. Once in his room, he called Daniel to review the days activities. It was never too late to call Daniel.

"Hello," Daniel said, as he picked up on the second ring.

"Hello, Daniel, how goes the battle?" Charles asked him cheerily.

"Fine, sir. As always. How was your day?"

"I think we can say victorious, Daniel. The two senators and I met with the governor late this afternoon, then we went to a dinner at the Convention Center. There were a thousand people there at $1,000 a plate. I'd say we did fantastic work for the party tonight. The governor assured me that we will carry the state in November. He suggested that we come to Los Angeles next month and hold another fund raiser."

"He's right. If we carry California, it could mean the election," Daniel answered.

Charles asked him, "How did your meeting go today with the group from the NRA? I know they were disappointed that I wasn't there."

"Yes, they were, but I told them that you would see them next week. Sorry, but I had to appease them somehow. We'll squeeze them in."

"I'll leave that up to you. I just swam laps for an hour, and I feel better than I have in years. I don't know why I stopped swimming."

"This morning, sir, Siefkin, what did he want that was so urgent?"

"Oh, that," Charles answered with a sigh. "I just put that out of my mind after he left. He said there might exist a tape or recording that would be damaging to me or my family. Apparently, it could be connected to the disappearance of an ex-agent with the CIA. Like I said, I haven't really thought about it. There is always someone threatening to expose details about me or Sarah or the children. If I worried about each incident, I would never leave my office."

Daniel's whole body was shaking now. "Did he give you the name of the agent?"

"I believe it was Saul Abrahms. I don't remember him. Why? Do you know him?"

"No. I just thought I might look into it. We can't be too careful."

"Security has been really tight here. There were seven agents watching me in the pool tonight."

"Like I said, we can't be too careful. There are a lot of nuts out there," Daniel added.

"I hear you, just glad you didn't say San Francisco," Charles answered with a laugh. "If you find out there is any truth to Siefkin's story, we can deal with it then. What else happened today? Did you see Sarah or the kids?"

"I spoke to Sarah briefly. She stopped by my office to check your schedule," he lied.
He could feel the sweat starting to run down his face. How long would it be until the FBI finds Saul and the tape? They chatted a few more minutes, which seemed like an eternity to Daniel, and finally he said, "I still have a lot of reading to do tonight, so I will give you a call in the morning."

"Fine," Charles answered, and they both hung up.

∞

As Karen drove away from the Retreat, she thought back on the last seven days. One Friday night she was packing for a trip to buy her engagement ring for her marriage to the man she truly loved, and who loved her as well, and now she was a terrified fugitive, running for her life. She knew what Daniel Slobe was capable of. He stopped at nothing to get what he wanted, and to wind up where he wanted to be. Charles Hamilton was not elected President only on his charm, good looks, and pedigree. Daniel had always worked behind the scenes to be sure that Charles had the backing of powerful groups and compelling people. Charles knew what Daniel did and how he operated, but he put it out of his mind, and went ahead as the man in front, untouched by any political scandal. Oddly, and luckily enough, Daniel also had not been implicated in any scandals related to Charles' campaigns, when he was a senator from Missouri, and now as President. How in the world had Daniel let this happen? Was he in love with Sarah Hamilton and had he let his passion for her ruin his whole life? Daniel would stop at nothing to keep this tape and affair from surfacing. I can't run forever, Karen thought. They will find me sooner or later.

Traveling 75 miles an hour on the freeway south, she considered what she had heard on the radio last night. President Hamilton was coming to San Francisco for some fund raising for the party, and all sorts of thoughts started running through her mind. He is staying two nights, she told herself. He doesn't know me well, but we met when I was assigned at the White House, and we were also introduced at the birthday party when Carrie turned fourteen. He must also know that I am engaged to Brian. Maybe I could meet with him and tell him about the tape. Then she realized this was crazy. How would she get in to see him? And, he might be just as ruthless as Daniel, and have her hauled away on the spot. But, maybe not. I could try and get to him, give him the facts, let him know what is in store for him. Or maybe I should contact Sarah. God, she thought, I wish I had never met Saul Abrahms. Saul, she wondered where he was.

The announcer from the news channel she had tuned in on the car radio started talking about the speech that the President was going to deliver this afternoon at the DeYoung Museum in Golden Gate Park. Her mind started spinning. She was 25 miles to the exchange which would take her to into Golden Gate Park. It was a long shot, but maybe she could somehow arrange a meeting with the President. She decided to try. She took the exit at Santos Creek, and headed West toward San Francisco. In 45 minutes she would be in Golden Gate Park, trying to secure a meeting with the President of the United States. How in the hell was she going to make this happen?

∞

Daniel, in his office, hung up the phone after talking to Acer Forbes, his contact in the CIA. Acer and Daniel had been working together for five years now, and understood each other perfectly. Daniel had an evil heart; Acer put it into practice. The people that Acer had hired to find Karen and the tape had failed so far.
"Acer," Daniel had said, "I don't need to tell you how critical this is to me and the President."

He had not told him the specifics, just that the tape was of national security, and of top secret in nature. If Acer suspected anything personal, he had not said it. Daniel was often secretive in his requests; and, the less Acer knew, the better. Acer was just following orders. And if people died, well, he had his orders. Daniel replayed his conversation with Acer in his mind.

"My people know that Karen was in Mexico, probably had the tape with her, but we haven't located her or the tape."

"Mexico?" Daniel questioned, "How the hell did she get to Mexico without us knowing it? Aren't we watching all the borders?"

"She must have gone before we started looking for her."

"You have an agent in Mexico now?" Daniel asked.

"Yes, and we have some good information regarding where Karen went and who she talked to."

"You know, don't you, that this has to remain totally under the fucking radar. If any of this gets out, we are fucked. Do we know if Karen is still there?"

"We think she is, but, if we haven't found her there after today, I will pull our operative and bring her home."

"Her?" Daniel asked.

"Don't worry. There isn't a sympathetic bone in this woman's body."

"I'm not condoning murder, Acer," Daniel said.

"No, of course not," Acer answered, knowing what a lie that was. "I will call you when I have more information."

"Do you have people in the States looking for Karen or Saul?"

"East Coast and West Coast. Something turned up in California, though. We might have a lead on Karen at a motel north of San Francisco."

"Jesus Christ, Acer. Is she in Mexico or California? What the fuck are you doing? You know that the President is giving a speech in San Francisco today."

"I remember, now that you say. I will follow up and let you know what we find out."

"Another thing, a private investigator named Winston Morris. Have you heard of him?"

"No. Want me to do some checking?"

"Yes. Find out where he is and let me know. I can't tell you again how critical this is to me, and to the President."

"I got it." Acer replied, but the line was dead.

Acer looked at the receiver then set it back on the cradle. This goes beyond anything Daniel has ever asked me to do. He wondered what was so critical. Critical or not, money paid by Daniel would fund into Acer's bank account in the Caymans. It's better that I don't know, he told himself.

As he dialed the number for Serge, he reflected on the past times he had worked for Daniel. Never before had he heard such a foul tone. Something was putrid. Something bad was happening or had happened already. Acer was curious, but not so curious as to jeopardize the flow of money into his account. Or so he thought. The phone call connected. Serge answered on the third ring.

"Hello, Acer," he said.

"What's going on? Have you got any news for me? Any good news?"

 "No. There's been a fuck up." Serge admitted.

"What? What are you talking about?"

"My girl, she lost her head and shot someone in Mexico"

"Why is this a fuck up? You shoot people all the time"

"I think the guy she shot knew where the tape was. I don't know exactly what happened. But I think she knew the guy from before. I think she knows Karen, too."   Serge knew perfectly well that Natalie knew Karen, but he wasn't telling Acer.

"Why the hell did she kill him, then?"

"It was an accident. They struggled, and her gun went off. Shot him right in the stomach."

"Jesus Christ, Serge.   You're shooting the people we need to find the tape. What about Karen?"

"We're pretty sure she is in Northern California. We traced her to a motel and know she was driving a red Mustang. We missed her at the motel, but talked to the manager, and she must have left there about 5:00 pm last night. We are looking up and down the coast, talking to anyone she knew in the past."

"I've got a bad feeling about this, Serge. She could be anywhere. And we still don't have the tape."

"Don't worry. We will find her. She can't stay off the radar forever."

"I don't have forever, Serge. Just find her, and the tape. And make sure the killing in Mexico is not linked to us in any way. I'll call you tomorrow. Have good news for me."

Chapter Nine

Karen sighed deeply as she took the exit for Golden Gate Park off highway 101. As she descended onto the tree-lined street, she saw the security ropes around the parking lot for the DeYoung Museum. She drove past the parking lot and found a place to park a mile down the narrow road. She got out of her car, locked the door and walked back toward the Museum. The parking lot. The lot was filled with secret service cars, at least that is what she assumed. All late model, dark sedans, American makes. As she scanned the lot, she saw that uniformed police were stationed about every 25 yards. I guess they can run 25 yards, she said to herself, if someone tries to run into the lot. At the edge of the lot she walked onto a grassy hill, and climbed up so she could see more clearly the lot and the entrance to the Museum. If anyone without credentials was getting in here, they would have to fly in on a helicopter. Now what do I do, she thought.

She crossed the street and started to walk along the perimeter of the park. She was going away from her destination, but she needed to think. She walked for ten minutes, but nothing came to her. Now she was at the intersection of Broadway and Fifth, one of the main entrances to the park. I'll walk back, she told herself, around the other side of the Museum, maybe then I'll have an idea. She walked through the

86

trees and the azaleas planted in the flower beds at the street and continued into the park again. This time she was on the north side of the building. There were security people on this side also. The parking had been blocked off on that side of the street, so no cars were there.

She kept walking, and suddenly, she saw a familiar face. It was Lotta Hernandez, a woman she had trained with when they both joined the FBI. Lotta had been assigned to security for the Vice President. She had either changed details, or they had added people here for this venue. I've got to talk to her, she thought. She took off her sunglasses and waved at Lotta. Lotta didn't see her at first, but then she looked at her and stared.

"Lotta, it's me, Karen," she yelled.

"Karen? What the hell are you doing here?"

'It's a long story. Can I talk to you for a minute?" Karen asked and gestured that she would come across the street.

Lotta looked around, at the other agents on that side of the building, then said, "Better not come over here. Security is pretty tight. I'll be leaving here in an hour, when the President is finished with the speech. We were sent here to secure the park. The city wanted extra help. We can talk somewhere before I get on the plane for D.C."

"What time is that?" Karen asked.

"About 3:00 pm."

"Are you at a hotel?" Karen asked her.

"No, we flew out this morning, took up our posts, and we are flying back this afternoon."

"I saw a Peet's Coffee at the entrance of Broadway and Fifth, that way," Karen pointed. "Can you meet me there in an hour?"

"I can, yes. You don't look so good. Is everything all right?"

"Everything's fine," she answered. "I just need a few minutes of your time."

"Peet's. I'll be there. I should get the okay to vacate this post shortly."

"And, Lotta," Karen said, "do come alone, please."

Lotta shook her head in agreement and watched as Karen turned back toward the entrance to the park. Strange, she thought. Karen Moss. What was she doing here? She worked fraud detail in Washington, and also at the White House, it was rumored. Maybe she was on vacation. No, she looked like hell. And, her hair, it was blonde.

One of the agents that Karen passed on her way out of the park walked towards Lotta and asked her, "Is everything all right? Any problems?"

"Oh, no. Just someone I knew from school. What a coincidence, huh?"

"Yea, small world."

At 1:15 pm, the President and his entourage emerged from the DeYoung, got into black limousines and drove out of the parking lot, heading for downtown San Francisco. The cadre of secret service from the area merged toward the sedans parked in the lot. Lotta found her car, and waited by the door as the senior agent approached and unlocked the trunk so she could retrieve her purse.

As she picked up her purse, she said to him, "I am going to walk to a store at the edge of the park. I told my mom I would bring her a souvenir from San Francisco. She's never been here, and she loves souvenirs. You know, maybe a little cable car, or a Golden Gate Bridge. It will probably be only 30 minutes. Do you mind waiting?"

She knew he wouldn't mind. He was famous for sleeping in his car. He had been on the job way too long. He kept a book and a flask in the glove compartment.

"No problem. Do you want me to drive you?"

"No. The walk will be good for my legs before the flight back to D.C. Can you just wait here?"

"You've got your cell?" he asked her.

"Sure.   Just call me if something comes up before I get back. Do you want something?"

"Nah. I'll just rest my eyes here for a minute." The other sedans pulled out of the lot, and if they noticed that Harris lagged behind, they didn't comment. He was always a little slow.

"I'll hurry." Lotta promised as she walked away. Harris didn't hear her though. He was already in the car, opening the glove compartment.

When Lotta came in the door of the coffee shop, Karen waved to her from a table in the back away from the window.   Lotta approached her and said, "Sitting in the back, away from the window. Now I know something's going on."

Karen looked at her, nodded slightly, then said, "Coffee? I got you one. Black, right?"

"Right. Spill, Karen," she said as she sat down.

"I only have a few minutes until I need to get back to the car. I told Harris I was getting souvenirs for my mom."

"I just wanted to know if you know where the President is staying in San Francisco tonight. What hotel?"

"The Sheraton Downtown is where he was last night. I guess he's still there. It would be a security hassle to move him for one more night. He has two more stops this afternoon, than a press conference at 6:00 pm, then a dinner at 8:00. Why do you ask?"

"I want to talk to him." Karen had decided to tell her as much of the truth as she could. "I know something of a personal nature that I think he should know before any of it hits the media."

Karen watched Lotta's face as she absorbed this information. Her eyes grew wide, but her face remained placid.

"Personal nature? What do you mean?" she asked Karen.

"I'm sorry, but I can't tell you. It's just imperative that I speak to him, alone."

"Karen, you and I both know that is next to impossible, really, it probably is impossible.

You'll never get near him. Especially at a hotel, tonight, in San Francisco."

"Well, now that you say hotel, me, a woman alone," Karen tilted her head coquettishly.

"Those are only rumors," Lotta admonished her. "There are no women in his hotel rooms when he is out of Washington."

"Yea, right. No women, ugly rumors." Karen answered.

"Now honestly, what are you up to? You look like shit, and you are hiding in a corner at Peet's, talking crazy. Tell me, what do you know? Maybe I can help?"

For a moment, Karen was tempted to tell Lotta everything. Lotta was resourceful, a friend, not too close, but she trusted her. But she knew she couldn't involve her in this mess. Then her life would be at risk also. It might already be, just by meeting Karen here today.

"Lotta," she began, "I wish I could tell you everything, but I can't. The less you know the better. In fact, why don't you buy your gifts and get back to the car. Seriously, you can't help me anymore than you already have."

Lotta remembered Karen from Quantico, she was stubborn and determined. If she wasn't sharing information, she wouldn't talk her into it. She stood up to go.

"I'm worried to leave you here alone," she said.

"No, you're not," Karen said, smiling. "You know I can take care of myself."

"Well, yes, but I'm still worried."

Lotta's phone beeped, and she looked at the message from Harris, who was anxious to get going. 'On my way', she answered.

"I've got to go, Karen. She pulled out one of her cards and a pen from her purse. She wrote something on the back of the card and gave it to Karen. My private phone is the reverse of the office. I don't tell everyone that. Call me."

"I will," said Karen. "I hope I will anyway. Go," she pointed to the door, "and thanks."

Lotta hurried to the door, fighting the urge to look back one last time at Karen, but exiting and running now toward the parking lot and the waiting car.

Karen sat alone at the table. She turned over the card and read what Lotta had written. "O'Shaunessy, Sheraton". Karen read the name over again. O'Shaunessey, Karen thought. Then she remembered. He was an agent they both knew from Washington. Divorced, not bad looking, always trying to date either one of them. Then going out with Lotta for a few months, until Lotta broke it off. O'Shaunessy, Karen said almost out loud. He must be with the President now. He'll be at the hotel. Thanks, Lotta, she mumbled and left the coffee shop. She walked to her car knowing she had seven or eight hours to come up with a plan and put it into action. She unlocked the car, started the engine, then drove out of the park, turning west toward downtown. The plan was beginning to come together in her head. Thank God for Lotta, she thought. She only hoped that O'Shaunessy remembered her. She would have little time for explaining.

Chapter Ten

As Karen was driving to the heart of downtown San Francisco, Serge was getting off a private jet in Zihuatanejo, Mexico. He looked over at a commercial plane where passengers were walking down the stairs into the bright Mexican sun. Summer's a lousy time to come down here, he told them in his mind. Way too hot. You should come to Mexico in the winter, when it is snowing in the states. Then the 80 degree weather is perfect. Summer heat in Mexico is intense, and besides it usually rains in the summer.

But that wasn't his problem now. He had come to see Natalie, to clean up any messes she left. He took his bag from the pilot and said, "I should be ready to leave in the morning. Meet me here at 10:00 am."

"Right.", answered the pilot, then turned and walked back up the stairs into the plane. His wife, also a pilot, leaned out the door and yelled at Serge, "Don't do anything I wouldn't do."

Serge waved back at her, "Don't worry. See you in the morning."

He then walked into the terminal, went through immigration, pushed the security bell, and being released to go, exited through the double doors into the blinding sun. There he got into one of the waiting taxis. "Downtown," he said to the young man. "And fast. Arribe." Serge had limited Spanish, and hoped he had said it right.

"Si, senor. Arribe, fast. Donde, where in the town do you want to go?"

"Hotel Florida." That is where Natalie had said she was staying, and they had arranged to meet there today, this afternoon.

"Si, senor," said the driver and left the parking area and entered the highway heading toward town, increasing his speed as he left the airport. Serge didn't say anymore, but rode in silence. Fortunately, the driver was quiet also. Serge needed to think. He had been constructing the chain of events while he was on the plane, actually ever since he had talked to Acer the last time. At first the mission seemed low priority, just find Karen and detain her for the FBI. Now, with the information that Natalie had, it became find Karen and eliminate her, but more importantly find this metal box and whatever is inside it. When they spoke, Acer was upset. I wonder what this is really about, he thought. Definitely something in Washington, D.C. He wondered how high up it went. Whatever it was, he was now determined to find Karen himself, and the metal box. He always worked alone in the beginning. He was smooth and secretive. He left no loose ends, or traceable evidence. His work was exact, and he never divulged any of his business. His reputation grew, and he took on operatives to help him. Natalie had been one of those operatives, and she had worked feverishly for the last three years. But now, something had gone wrong. I should never have asked her to find Karen, he told himself. Too much history there.

After twenty minutes, the cab pulled in front of a white stucco building, three stories high, facing the town square and church.

"Hotel Florida," the driver announced. He stepped out of the cab and retrieved Serge's bag from the trunk. Serge also got out of the cab carrying a smaller bag, and asked the driver, "Cuantos?"

"One hundred sixty pesos," he told him. Serge handed him two hundred from a roll of pesos he had in the front pocket of his jeans.

"Gracias," said the driver with a smile.

"De nada." Serge answered, and turned toward the entrance of the hotel. He picked up his larger bag and went inside. He scanned the lobby. A man and a woman were standing by the elevator, and there was a woman behind the counter.

"Hola, senor," she said.   "Bien venidos. Welcome to the Hotel Florida. Would you like a room?"

"I am looking for someone who is staying here, a friend. Her name is Natalie Hunter."

"Ah, si, Miss Hunter. Quite a beautiful lady. But she left this morning."

"This morning? Are you sure? Did you see her go?"

"Si. I am the only one here at this desk today. Summer is very slow for us in this town. The tourists go to Ixtapa."

"Did she say where she was going? Did you talk to her at all before she left?"

"Not this morning. She merely turned in her key and left. But yesterday we talked briefly. She was going to the dive shop at the end of the pier. She was friends with Alessandro." Her face darkened, and she continued somberly. "Alessandro was shot and killed yesterday, in his rooms. She was very upset by this as she had been with him in his boat only the day before."

"She knew him?" Serge questioned.

"She said she had met him in the United States, in California."

98

"What else did she tell you?"

"Nada. Just small words. It seemed they were friends. She went out on Alessandro's boat, I think. She didn't talk much about it. She left word only to find her in the hotel if Alessandro or Manuel called for her."

"Manuel? Who is he?" Serge asked.

"Alessandro's friend. He worked with him. I feel so sorry for him. I don't know what he will do now. Alessandro took care of him and his family."

"You say she went to a pier yesterday?"

"Si. She went there both of the days she was here, not today, though. Today she left in a hurry."

"Did she say where she was going?"

"We did not talk, senor. Miss Hunter, she took some breakfast in the sunroom, and then checked out."

"Can you guide me to the pier where she went?"

"Si. Go to the end of the city beach, then go around the small hotel that sits at the end of the beach. Keep walking and you will see the small pier, and the dive shop where Alessandro had his business. Just go outside and get a taxi. Tell the driver you want to go to Alessandro's dive shop. Everyone knows it. Will you be coming back? Do you want a room?"

"No. I won't be staying now. Gracias." Serge put two hundred pesos on the desk and turned to go.

Outside, he found a taxi. Serge told the driver he wanted to go to the dive shop of Alessandro. The driver nodded his head, and opened the door for Serge to get into the back seat. As they drove the short five minutes to the city beach, Serge contemplated Natalie's disappearance. Natalie was not stupid. On the contrary, she was very smart and educated in the ways of the hired killer. Kill or be killed. Natalie knew she was expendable. She had not found Karen. And now she probably knew too much. Damn, he thought, I played this one wrong. It was just all happening too fast. And even he did not know what was really going on. He just knew it was big.

Why am I going to this place? he asked himself. Before he could answer in his head, the taxi stopped, and the driver said, "We are here. The shop of Alessandro."

Serge looked out the window and saw a small building sitting at the end of the beach with the bay stretching out to the Pacific Ocean. A beautiful spot, but he had neither the time nor the inclination to enjoy it.

"Please wait for me here," he said to the driver and got out of the car. "Momento. I'll be back in a minute."

"Si, senor. I will wait."

Serge walked to the structure and went in through the open doorway. He had to step over fins, masks, glasses, suntan lotions and bottles of water scattered over the floor. Someone had stripped the shelves looking for something. He walked into the back area and saw again that papers and t-shirts were laying on the floor. Natalie, he thought. I wonder if she found what she was looking for. He turned to leave when he heard a small whimper in the back corner of the room. Moving a chair and air mattress, he found a small boy, eyes red and wet, staring up at him.

"Hola," he said quietly. The child hovered deeper into the corner. "It's okay," Serge said gently. "What are you doing here?"

The child only looked at him.

"Come with me," he said and motioned to the front of the shop. No movement.

"Venga con me."

Still no movement from the child. Serge reached down and took the small boy's arm and lifted him to his feet. "It's okay. Venga."

Standing, the child stiffened his body, and Serge picked him up and carried him from the shop. He took him to the taxi and said to the driver.

"Ask him what he was doing in the dive shop?"

"Por que estas en la tienda?"

"Estoy esperando a Alessandro. Que desayuno," the boy answered.

"He's waiting for Alessandro. For breakfast."

Serge felt pity for the boy. "Tell him Alessandro is not coming. He won't be coming anymore."

The driver translated to the boy, who looked doubtful and scared at the same time.

"Here," Serge said, and handed the boy a wad of pesos from his pocket. "Take these home to your mother."

The boy took the money, and stared at Serge.

"Go, now. Go home," he said, and threw his arm in the direction of the town. Then, he stopped himself and grabbed the boy by the arm. He said to the driver, "Ask him if he saw anyone else at the shop this morning."

"Nadie estaba en la tienda esta manana?"

"No," the boy answered, and jerked his arm from Serge's grip. Then he began running away from the taxi down the road toward the square. Serge watched him for a moment, then before he got in the taxi, he noticed the open air bar across from the dive shop.

"Wait here," he told the driver. "I am going to talk to the bartender."

"Si, senor," said the driver, and picked up the newspaper laying on the front seat.

Serge approached the open air bar and took a seat near the end. The bartender came over and asked him what he wanted to drink. Putting one hundred pesos on the bar, Serge said, "Just a few questions. Do you speak English?"

"Yes."

"Do you know Alessandro and Manuel, from the dive shop?"

"Si. It is terrible what happened. Who would do such a thing? Everyone loved Alessandro, especially Manuel."

"When did you see Alessandro last?"

"Yesterday. He was at his shop in the morning, then he left. He didn't go diving as usual. Then, well, the tragedy."

"And Manuel, did you see him yesterday?"

"No. But the day before Manuel and a woman went with Alessandro out to the sea to dive."

"A woman with black hair?"

"Si. Bella."

"Did you see her yesterday or today?"

"I saw her last night. She was walking on the beach, alone."

"You didn't talk to her?"

"No. I saw her go by in the direction of town."

"Gracias," Serge said and left the bar. He walked quickly to the taxi and opened the back door and got inside. "Al aeropuerto," he told the driver. Then he removed his cell and placed a call to Acer.

As the taxi drove to the turn which entered the highway going toward the airport, the small boy ran up the hill to his home. He ran through the open air living room and pulled back the cloth curtain which hid his small bed and wooden chest where he kept his few possessions. He opened the bottom drawer of the chest and removed a metal box with a beautiful jeweled lid. He lifted the lid and placed the wad of pesos that the stranger had given him into the box. Then he replaced the box in the drawer and pushed it shut. He then left his home and started walking back down the hill. He missed Alessandro and wondered why he had given him the box, with instructions to tell no one that he had it.

Chapter Eleven

After a sleepless night, Sarah Hamilton got out of bed at 5:00 am. She ran a bath as usual, called for coffee, but she could barely function for thinking of the tape and the situation now with Daniel. She picked up her phone and dialed again Daniel's cell, but just like the prior calls she made at 2:00 am, 3:00 am, and 4:00 am, there was no answer. Obviously, he was not going to talk to her. She sat down at her desk, drinking her first cup of coffee, and considered her options. If this story broke, they would all be finished. She looked at her shaking hands, and longed for the brandy under the sink in the bathroom. Not today, she told herself. I can't do it today. She got up and changed from her gown to running shorts and a tee shirt. She found her tennis shoes in the back of her closet and put them on with a pair of thick socks. Then she dialed from the house phone to secret service, telling the agent who answered that she was going for a run, and to be ready to meet her at the outside door of the kitchen.

She knew if she stayed any longer in her room, she would pour that brandy into the coffee, and begin another day of drifting and dreaming, and sinking to that level of nothingness, where she could never have seen herself fifteen years ago. It had been fifteen years, before Carrie was born, that she ran each morning, and today, she told herself, she needed to start again.

Outside the kitchen entrance to the White House, two agents dressed in running gear waited for the First Lady. Another two agents waited in separate black cars at the street.
Sarah came downstairs and went through the kitchen, smiling at the staff, then opened the door and greeted the two men waiting there.

"Shocking, isn't it?" she said to them. They just looked at her, dumfounded. "I mean, I haven't run in years. But I guess you never knew me then did you?" she said merrily.

"No, Mrs. Hamilton," answered one of the men.

Seeing that they were just waiting for her lead, she began with a slow trot to the edge of the driveway, then started down the drive to the streets of Washington, D.C. The two men followed closely behind, and one of the cars proceeded to get in front of them, while the other stayed behind. Sarah was winded after three blocks, but she forced herself to keep going. She couldn't even feel her hands shaking after ten blocks. After running 20 minutes, she stopped and bent over. Immediately, the two agents came to her and one of them asked if she was all right.

"Just tired," she said and held her side.

"Do you want to ride back?" one of the men asked her.

She thought for a moment, then answered, "No, but I'll start back now."

Then she turned in the direction of the White House and resumed running. Her side hurt, she could barely breathe, and all she could think about was a drink.

In 30 minutes she was again in her room, this time with a tall glass of ice water, and dialing Daniel's number for the fifth time. Still, he would not answer. She went into her bathroom, felt the bath water, now cold, and let it out of the tub. She started a shower, removed her clothes, and stepped in. This morning was different. Maybe everything would be okay after all.

∞

Daniel looked at his phone as it vibrated. Five am. Sarah again. He knew he would have to talk to her sometime, he just couldn't do it now. A meticulous planner, he normally did not panic. How, then, had he become involved with the President's wife? Such a temptation, such a pleasure, but now, his life could be over. If he didn't have Charles, he had nothing. He would go nowhere else in politics or private life with this scandal over him. He searched for someone to blame, Sarah? Charles? Himself? Am I just human, he asked himself. Everyone called him a machine, with no feelings, and, true, that is usually how he acted. Mercilessly, ruthlessly, to get what he wanted, and what he had wanted was for Charles Hamilton to be President of the United States, and he Chief of Staff. Now that he had succeeded in his life's quest, he was set to fall harder, faster, and with more cruelty than anyone he had ever dealt with. Feeling nostalgic and vulnerable for a moment, he remembered his longings for Sarah starting fifteen years ago, when he first went to work with Charles on a campaign for governor. But he was smarter then, more directed.

When Charles became President, he and Sarah both were relegated to the background. Perhaps it was beyond their control that they would fall together and love each other. He thought about the feel of Sarah in his arms for just a moment, then stopped himself and saw where he was today. If this story gets out, he might as well be dead. He dialed Acer's number, hoping to get good news.

Acer answered, and they spoke briefly. Acer had sent his best people to Mexico, looking for Karen, but the news was not good. He hadn't located Karen or the tape. He was also looking for Saul, who seemed to disappear from the planet. After speaking to Acer, Daniel knew that he was hoping for a miracle. There was a tape which Sarah had given to Saul who had given it back to Sarah. Saul had given a copy to Karen, so they thought. Maybe they were after the wrong people, and Saul would have made other copies of the tape, wouldn't he? Surveillance was his business. How Saul could let this opportunity for blackmail pass him by, Daniel could not fathom. Maybe I should just get on a plane today for South America, and never come back, he thought. I could just quit today. Disappear like Saul had. No, he told himself. Acer would find Karen, and she would have the tape. They could use Karen as a pawn to get to Saul.

Daniel showered, dressed, and left for his office, as he did every morning except for Christmas. As he started his car, his phone vibrated again in his pocket. He didn't even look at it this time. Just a few more hours, Sarah. He would call her with news.

A few hours passed, and Daniel sat in his office, unable to concentrate, and finally the phone rang. Picking up his cell, he saw it was Acer.

"Hello," Daniel answered.

"Daniel, I don't have good news."

"Go on," Daniel said.

"Our operative, the one we sent to Mexico to find Karen and the tape, well, she has left there and flown to San Francisco. This morning."

"Does she have the tape? Did she find Karen?"

"She did not find Karen, and we are not sure about the tape."

"What do you mean not sure about the tape? Do you know if she had it?"

"We found out that she might have had it in Mexico, but where it is now, we can't be sure."

"Jesus Christ, Acer. What the fuck is can't be sure'? Tell me what you do know."

"Like I said, we have an operative we sent to Mexico. She got into some trouble and left, but before she left, she might have seen a box with the tape in it. Or so she thought."

"This isn't making any sense. If she thought the tape was there, why didn't she secure it?"

Acer struggled to explain to Daniel what Serge had told him earlier. There had been a major fuck up when Natalie killed Alessandro, the one person who knew where the tape might be.

"It's complicated," he said. "Things happened. She wound up killing the only person who might have known where the tape was."

Daniel was silent for a moment, then it hit him, and he said, "San Francisco. The President is in San Francisco. Holy Christ almighty. Your woman must have the tape."

111

"Daniel," Acer finally asked, "what is on this tape?"

"It involves the President. That's all I can say. It will be destructive, damaging, harmful, to him and the country if it comes out."

"What kind of damage, what is so harmful to require all this secrecy and murder? Who else is involved with the President?"

"I can't say anymore. Just know that we have to find this tape and keep this information from going public. I've paid you enough, Acer. Just do your fucking job. You need to find your operative before she gets to the President."

 "I have my best man on his way to San Francisco now. Tell me the President's exact schedule for today."

Daniel detailed the movements of the President for the day, ending with the dinner at a private residence at 8:00 pm.

"Don't worry. We will keep this woman away from the President. We will find her and see what she knows."

"Do you have people in Hamilton's security detail?" Daniel asked.

"Just don't worry. If anyone tries to get near Charles Hamilton, we will be ready."

All the while he was talking to Acer, Daniel keep thinking about his affair with Sarah. Was it worth it? Sadly, he didn't know the answer. After hanging up from Acer, he phoned transportation and scheduled a flight to San Francisco. If Charles finds out about this tonight, I am going to be there, he told himself.

∞

Stepping from the shower, Sarah Hamilton also knew that today was a turning point in her life. If everything was over, she was going to face it all sober. Daniel, obviously was lost to her. But, maybe she could keep Charles. She wrapped herself in a towel and went to her desk where she dialed her secretary and instructed her to arrange a flight to San Francisco. She was going to surprise Charles.

"Is it a special occasion?" Martha asked her.

"No, I just feel like surprising him for once," she answered.

∞

Karen had driven from Golden Gate Park to the Sheraton Hotel. She trusted Lotta that President Hamilton was staying here tonight, and the existence of the security check booth she went

113

through to enter the hotel told her it was true. She went to the front counter and checked into a room, using the name of Natalie Hunter, her best friend from high school. Certainly, she thought, Natalie would not be here tonight. She carefully avoided making eye contact with anyone in the lobby, as the place was crawling with secret service agents. Even though she had blonde hair now and was dressed radically different from the Karen that worked in Washington, she still worried that one of the men or women in the lobby would recognize her.

After getting her card key, she immediately went to her room on the eleventh floor. Opening the door, she could see that the windows looked out over the bay. It was a stunning view. The day was perfectly clear, and she could see the Golden Gate Bridge before her. She thought just for a moment how romantic it would be if she were here with Brian.

Reality returned quickly, however, and she began getting ready to put her plan into action. She put on a large pair of sunglasses, then left her room for the elevator. She rode to the lobby and went out the front doors into the city. She would find a shop where she could buy a sexy outfit, something that would attract the eye of the President of the United States when he returned from his dinner this evening. She knew from past accounts that he would be relaxed after his usual cocktails and wine with dinner, and perhaps vulnerable to a young, attractive woman. As she walked through the lobby, she looked for O'Shaunessy, but she didn't see him. If he wasn't in the lobby later tonight, her plan might not work.

After walking a few blocks, she found a boutique and purchased a red dress which hugged her figure and showed a healthy view of her breasts. She also bought a pair of red 4" heels which accentuated her legs. Next she located a salon and had her hair and make-up done. She emerged from the shop as a white platinum blonde with glowing cheeks and seductive eyes. Looking in the mirror behind the counter as she paid, she didn't even recognize herself.

∞

At 7:00 PM that evening, President Hamilton and his entourage left the Sheraton to travel to the house on Nob Hill where a wealthy patron was hosting the $10,000 a plate dinner in support of the party. The dinner officially started at 8:00, but Charles was never late. He made it a habit to be early. He hated tardiness in himself and anyone around him. Security in the hotel was extremely tight, and at least twenty agents strolled the lobby before he left and during his departure. After he was gone, ten remained, with the other ten joining the President for the short ride to Nob Hill. Charles was wearing a tux, and looked extremely handsome, his dark features highlighted by the crisp white shirt. The swimming he had undertaken was helping his weak back, and for the first time in many weeks, he felt splendid. He knew nothing could go wrong this evening. He was at the height of his popularity and in step to win a second term as President of the United States.

What he didn't know, however, was that at the very moment he was getting out of his limousine for the dinner, with cameras flashing and microphones held aloft, and crowds of people held back by security, his whole world was about to come crashing down around him. Four people were now conspiring in their own way to upend his life.

His wife Sarah was in a limousine on her way to his hotel. Daniel was already there waiting to speak to Charles. Karen was in her room trying on the red dress and the 4" heels with which she hoped to seduce him, and Serge was standing at the front desk of the Sheraton, questioning a clerk about the presence of a Natalie Hunter.
"Do you have a Natalie Hunter checked in tonight?" he asked the tall, young man.

The clerk looked at him briefly, then typed the name into his keyboard. "Yes, she checked in this morning."

"What room is she in?" Serge asked him quickly, hoping to catch him off guard.

"I can't tell you that, sir," he answered.

Serge considered putting a $100 bill on the counter, but he didn't want to draw any extra attention to himself. He had entered through the security booth, and took notice of the many plain clothed agents stationed throughout the lobby. So he left the hotel, deciding on another plan of action.

∞

The real Natalie Hunter had arrived from Mexico earlier in the day, and was checked into the Hilton. She still didn't know why she had chosen San Francisco. But there was a powerful force which drew her here. She knew she was a dead woman if she had stayed in Mexico. Whatever it was that Karen had, powerful people wanted, and Natalie had failed to get it. And, she had killed a man who had information, a friend, and for what? She was now expendable.

She poured herself the rest of the Zinfandel and considered the last few days. Serge had called her for a special, top secret job. This did not surprise her, as all her jobs were special and top secret. But Serge had been more anxious about this one. In the three years that she had been a paid assassin for Serge, she had never known the mark or any of the circumstances surrounding the target. And always, Serge was very matter of fact, with details of the target's life mailed to Natalie to a post office box with the instructions, always in code. The subject of our investigation was the target. Dates for the hit were coded weeks in advance, with each day being something else. Never was anyone else to be involved or harmed in the operation. Everything about their operation was clean and tidy. Her pay was wired into a bank in Switzerland. She in fact had a house there now, and planned to move there in a few years.

Her plans, though, changed with the call from Serge for this job. This job went against all her sensibilities, those that she still allowed herself to feel. Serge could have sent someone else to Mexico, but he needed someone who knew Karen and Alessandro When Serge asked her if she could follow through and complete the mission, even if it meant harming a friend, Natalie did not hesitate. "Of course," she told him, knowing, however, that she could never hurt Karen. But if someone wanted Karen dead, Natalie wanted to know why. She loved Karen. She always had. To Natalie, Karen was perfect, smart, beautiful, and honest. What you saw was what you got.

Killing Alessandro had been a mistake, an accident. But she could have prevented it. At times she felt as if a demon were living inside of her, a monster over which she had no control. These years of killing had changed her. At times, she sensed the old Natalie, but then she returned to the personality which allowed her to continue her work, masking any genuine feelings she had from the past.

Why did Serge pick me, she pondered. He needed someone Karen trusted, someone she would confide in. He knew that Natalie and Karen were best friends in high school, college, and beyond, and Natalie had shared with him stories of the times they spent together with Alessandro in Monterey when Karen was teaching there. That must be it. Karen had information on someone, and Serge knew she had gone to Mexico. He must have investigated further and found out that Alessandro had moved back to Mexico a few years after Karen left Monterey. Perhaps she had gone to see him. Finding out about the metal box had been a coincidence. Serge had not mentioned it when he gave Natalie the assignment, but now that she had told Serge about, it was imperative that they find it. Natalie remembered the metal box from Karen's dresser. It was beautiful, with a jeweled lid made of shiny stones. Karen's father had bought it for Karen in Spain and brought it home to her when she was only thirteen years old. Karen kept her deepest treasures in it.

The last time Natalie had spoken to Karen was at her brother's funeral, and that was only for a few short minutes. Natalie did not like being in her home town. Her life was too different now. Karen seemed fine then, happy with her job in the FBI and in love with a man she met in

Washington, ready to get married and have babies. "Pretty soon you'll be talking about cooktops and ovens," Natalie had kidded Karen. In high school, they swore they would never be concerned with kitchen appliances. "That won't be me," Karen had told her. "I'm getting married so he will be in my bed every night."

When Serge contacted Natalie and explained the little about the job he would disclose on the phone, Natalie sensed in him a heightened emotion. Normally, preternaturally calm, he seemed uneasy, and she noticed a raised pitch in his voice. Either he has second thoughts about Karen as a target, or there was an unusual amount of money involved. Perhaps it was both. Serge had lusted for Karen all through high school, competing with her in all their advanced classes. Karen narrowly surpassed him in her grades to become valedictorian, but Serge never accepted it. Maybe he was eager about this job so he could finally get back his own after all those days of watching Karen's success.

Or, it could have been the money. He was obsessed with money, even though he must be a multi-millionaire by now. With what he paid Natalie, he must get ten times that amount. For this job, he promised her half a million, and had already wired $100,000 into her account. But deep down, Natalie knew this was about Serge's long standing resentment.

Karen was with the FBI in Washington, D.C., had been for three years now. Her fiancé Brian was the assistant to the chief of staff for the President. Karen had disappeared from Washington a week ago, and surfaced once in Mexico with Alessandro. With her she had the metal box, which she tossed into the Pacific Ocean. Then she mysteriously gave Alessandro instructions to find it. Perhaps, there was some kind of scandal in Washington, which Brian had confided in her. Natalie poured herself another glass of wine, and reached for the newspaper resting beside her on the couch. On the front page was a picture of Charles Hamilton, leaving the Sheraton Hotel. Natalie started reading the article under the picture. The President was in San Francisco for the next two days doing fund raising for the candidates for Governor and Senator of his party.

At once she knew it. Karen was here in San Francisco. Alessandro had mentioned the President that morning she found him on the beach before the dive. Alessandro said that Karen was concerned for the safety of the President and his family. She thought it was strange that Karen had spoken to Alessandro about the President, and she had continually wondered what Hamilton had to do with this whole mystery.

That is why Natalie picked the flight from Mexico this morning to San Francisco. Something is going down with the President, and Karen knows what it is. She must have some kind of proof on that tape which Natalie did not find. She read further down, and learned that the President was at the Sheraton until tomorrow, and also that he was attending a dinner this evening at a home on Nob Hill. Natalie immediately rose from the couch and pulled clothes from her suitcase to change. When she was dressed all in black, she took her revolver and cartridges from her suitcase and placed them in her bag. Before she opened the door to the hall, she took a last look in the mirror, clear eyes, pretty face, broken heart.

Chapter Twelve

In her hotel room on the eleventh floor, Karen put on the red dress and the 4" heels she had purchased to lure the President. She expected him to notice her in the lobby after he came down to get into his car. His limousine would be parked in the front. She knew he wouldn't leave by a back entrance. That wasn't his style. He liked the attention, and the press would be all over the entrance to the hotel.

She looked in the mirror, fluffed up the back of her hair, checked her lipstick, and said to herself, yes, this is about as good as it is going to get. And not bad, either. Her hair was pulled seductively back behind one ear, and the red heels added four inches to her height. And she certainly wasn't carrying any extra weight, as over the last week, she had hardly eaten. Eating and thinking you are going to be killed just did not mix. She didn't want to hang out too long in the lobby, so she waited until 7:15 pm to go to the elevator and ride down. Exiting the elevator, she noticed that the lobby was rather quiet. Not a scene anticipating the arrival of the President. She walked past the desk and slowed down so she could look out the windows into the street. There were no cars outside. Either the President hadn't come down, or he had already left. She perused the lobby and noticed only five men in suits. He must be gone, she told herself. In looking at the men, however, she recognized

O'Shaunessy. He was standing about ten feet from the entrance. She immediately walked towards him. He watched as she approached, noting the platinum hair and the long legs. Karen stopped in front of him and quietly said his name.

"O'Shaunessy, right?"

He did not reply immediately, but just looked at her quizzically.

"You are Agent O'Shaunessy, aren't you?" she said again, quietly.

"I am Jack O'Shaunessy. Do I know you?"

Relieved, Karen continued. "We have never formally met, but I am a friend of Lotta Hernandez. We went through the academy together."

"Lotta," he looked surprised. "I haven't talked to her in two years."

"I know," Karen said. "But you dated, right?"

"We did," he said wistfully.

Karen watched his face and said, "I saw Lotta just today. She was working security for the President at the DeYoung, on special detail.

She is the one who told me I might find you here tonight."

"What is your name?" he asked her.

"Karen, Karen Moss."

"Are you on some kind of special detail, Karen?" he asked as his eyes moved from her head to her toes. "Are you still with the Bureau?"

"Yes, I am. And, uh, yes I am on an elite kind of mission. That is why I need your help tonight. Can we go somewhere and talk?"

"Well, the President is gone, just left, and we can, I mean, I guess I could leave this post for thirty minutes or so. We can go to the coffee shop in the hotel. I just need to let the others know I will be gone for a while. Why don't you go ahead and get a table. I will be in right away."

"Thanks," she told him and walked away toward the coffee shop. She entered the restaurant and was seated at a table in the further most corner of the room. Jack came in about five minutes later and was escorted by the hostess to Karen's table.

"Is this some kind of secret mission?" he asked.

"Extremely," she answered.

The waitress appeared, and they both ordered coffee. "Are you eating?" he asked her.

"Not yet, but, please, you go ahead."

"I'll have scrambled eggs and toast. Dry, rye," he told the waitress.

"Anything else?" the dark-haired girl asked.

"No, that will be it," he said.

The waitress left and returned with two cups of steaming coffee and left the cream on the table. "I'll have those eggs in just a few minutes," she said to Jack.

"Thanks," said Jack. "Now, Karen, tell me what is going on. Is this something to do with the President? If so, I don't know anything about it. I mean, there's been no word come down to us of anything suspicious."

She looked at him and sighed. "You wouldn't know," she told him. "In fact, no one knows anything about it, except me. Well, no, that's not true. It's a long story, and really I can only tell you a part of it. I just need you to trust me."

He looked into her eyes, and she returned the gaze.

"Lotta said you could help me."

Softening, he said, "Tell me, then, as much as you can. How can I help you?"

"There has been a situation," she began, "that compromises the President and his wife. A personal scandal, which I discovered about a week ago." As she spoke, she scanned the room. Jack followed her eyes. Then she continued.

"I was contacted by someone who had in his possession a tape which recorded a rendezvous, an explicitly sexual assignation, by a man and a woman extremely close to the President. I can't tell you anymore, but I must stress, that if this tape goes public, we will witness a scandal like Washington has never seen before."

"You have this tape?" he questioned.

"Not with me. It is in a safe place. I need to talk to the President. I know it sounds crazy, but it is imperative that I tell him about the tape before it becomes public."

"I thought the tape was in a safe place," Jack said.

"Yes, my copy is, but I don't know if there is another one somewhere. And there might be."

"How did you get this tape?"

"A friend came to me with it. I wish to God he hadn't, but it's too late now."

"A friend, who?"

"I'm sorry, Jack, I can't tell you. After he came to my apartment and we viewed the tape together, I told him to get out of the country. I kept the tape, but I don't know if he made a copy or not. I do know that he is not the type to use the tape for gain. He won't be blackmailing anyone, but if I give you his name, he will be in danger. Just like I am now. And, there is, according to him, a copy of the tape with one of the parties involved. I left Washington over a week ago. I have been on the run ever since. Seeing Lotta was just a break, a coincidence that led me to you."

Jack watched her as she spoke. He was kind hearted and understood people. He pictured Lotta, and those four months they spent together flooded his memory. He knew he would help this friend of hers.

"What is it you need from me?"

"I need to speak to the President in private, just him and me. I must tell him about the tape and hope he can do something about it. I just don't want it to become public before he knows about it."

The waitress then arrived with Jack's eggs and toast and set the plate before him.

"Anything else I can get you?" she asked.

"More coffee," he said.

The waitress filled their cups with the pot of coffee she held in her left hand. After she left, Karen continued.

"I want you to arrange for the President to come to my room in the hotel tonight."

Jack looked at her and rolled his eyes.

"I know about him. I've heard the stories of him and other women. He likes girls. That's fine. I'm not married to him. But tonight, I want to be one of those girls. I need him alone in my room, just him and me, after he returns from dinner."

"Jesus," Jack said, "I'm not that close to him. I've never set up any women before."

"But you know people who have, right?"

"Well, yes."

"Then set this up. Jack, if this information, which involves his wife, becomes public, the President is through. There will be no second term."

"I must be crazy," he told her, "but I believe you. And I will talk to someone who is privy to the President's activities, and try to arrange a meeting. I can't guarantee anything. What room are you in?"

A flow of relief spread through Karen's limbs. "1102", she told him. "I'll go there now and wait. Would you call my room when he gets back to the hotel?"

"Sure. But, this is only a maybe. I don't know what will happen when he returns. I will talk to someone and try to set it up, and truthfully, I've seen it happen in the past, but, like I said, I can't guarantee anything."

"Just try, Jack. Just try."

"Whatever happens, I will call you later tonight."

"I need to get back to my room," she said and stood up. "I'll wait for your call. And, thank you." She touched him on the shoulder, then turned and left the restaurant, walking quickly to the elevator. Part one of her plan had worked. Now, if the President cooperated, part two could be set into motion.

After Karen left the restaurant, Jack finished his meal and thought about what had just transpired. When he and Lotta split up, he had a feeling she would come back into his life. He just never imagined it would be like this.

Chapter Thirteen

Disappointed, but not defeated, Serge turned away from the reception desk and headed for the door. As he exited the lobby, he noticed again the security booth set up because of the President's visit. Tough to get a firearm in here, he said to himself. He would definitely need help from Acer for this. Once outside, he realized he had not eaten since early morning in Mexico. At the side of the entrance, near the entrance to the underground parking, was the podium of the valet captain. Serge approached the young man standing there, and asked, "Can you tell me where I could get a sandwich and a beer?"

The young man looked up from his computer screen and surveyed Serge. "Sure," he answered, "right around the corner. Just walk to the end of this block, and there is a small bar, Nicolo's. It's on the right hand side of street."

"Thanks," Serge told him and dropped a $20 bill on the podium. Serge walked to the corner and turned to find the restaurant. He entered and took a table toward the inside of the bar. He ordered a turkey sandwich and a lite beer. He ate quickly and left the bar within 20 minutes. He walked back toward the hotel where he had just left, and the same man was standing at his valet podium. Serge approached him again. "Hi there," he said. "The bar, Nicolo's, it was a good place. Thank you."

"No problem," the man answered.

Serge remained in front of the podium. "I'm hoping you can help me in another way. My girlfriend is staying at this hotel, and I want to surprise her. She didn't think I was going to get off work and meet her, but I managed to get away early. So, I don't know what room she is in. Can you tell me?"

Serge removed a $100 bill from his jacket pocket and placed it on the podium. The valet looked at the money, then at Serge. He hesitated, sighed, picked up the money, and asked, "What is her name?"

"Hunter. Natalie Hunter."

The valet typed in the name on his keyboard. Serge waited. "1102. And you didn't get it from me. You know the President is staying here tonight."

"Really?" Serge answered, trying to sound surprised. "Maybe we will run into him?"

"I doubt it. He is pretty heavily guarded."

"Well, no matter. We just want to be together. Probably won't leave the room. Thanks again."

Serge turned and walked to the entry doors and went through the security booth. He emptied his pockets and took off his shoes. It was just like flying.

"Come on through, buddy," the man on the other side of the table told him.

"Thanks."

Serge walked directly to the elevator and pressed the "up" button. The elevator arrived in a moment, and Serge was thankful it was empty. Maybe the hotel was not too full because of the President. But why let anyone else stay here, Serge thought, but on the other hand, they just couldn't close down this huge hotel for the President.

Inside the car, Serge pushed the button for floor 11, and the doors closed. The elevator sped to the eleventh floor. The doors opened, and Serge exited and looked for the signage on the wall directing him to number 1102. It was close to the elevator, on the right hand side of the hallway. He walked to the door, and stood there for a moment. Maybe Natalie was not in the room, and if she was, would she let him in? Would she call security? He knocked softly three times on the metal door. Then he waited. He thought he heard footsteps near the door. He knocked again, three times. He could sense someone looking at him.

In fact, on the other side of the door, Karen was looking through the peephole with disbelief. Was that really Serge Pachenko on the other side of the door? She had not seen him since high school. What was he doing here? Looking for Natalie, she thought instantly. I booked the room under her name.

Karen removed the security latch and opened the door slowly. She peeked her head around the door. "Serge?" she said hesitantly.

"Karen?" Serge replied. He practically fell off his feet. The blonde hair, the heavy make-up, but it looked like Karen.

"It's me. What are you doing here?"

"What are you doing here? I thought this was Natalie's room," he told her. Can I come in?"

"Come on in," Karen answered, and opened the door wider, all the while feeling anxious at this surprise appearance of her old high school rival. And, why was he looking for Natalie?

Serge, on the other hand, was feeling ecstatic. He wondered if he was smiling too broadly. The mystifying Karen, the woman he had been paid to find, and who had eluded him in two countries, was right here in this hotel, in this very room. He wondered again if Natalie and Karen were in this together. He entered the room and closed the

135

door after himself. Then he reached for the security latch and pushed it back to its locked position. Karen eyed him carefully. She backed away toward the window, still watching him.

"Quite a view," Serge commented and strolled over to the plate glass window, all the time watching Karen from the corner of his eye.

"Well, I gotta tell ya," Karen spoke as nonchalantly as she could muster, "I never in a gazillion years expected to see you here tonight. I haven't seen you since graduation. No I take it back, the class reunion. What are you doing here? How did you know I would be here?"

"I didn't know you would be here. I thought Natalie was here," he told her again. "I was looking for Natalie. She works for me."

Karen walked over to the small couch on the side of the room and stood behind it. She looked over at Serge in disbelief. "Natalie works for you? And, Serge, what is it exactly that you do?"

Karen had heard from people in the FBI that a Serge Pachenko was operating a criminal business, probably paid assassinations, but she had never believed it. And now, to hear that Natalie worked for him as well. She was in shock.

"My business, Karen," Serge replied slowly, "is finding people, and dealing with unpleasant situations which others don't want to handle. I handle them."

"Handle?" she spoke. "You mean you kill people. You're a paid assassin."

He pulled the chair out from the desk and sat down facing Karen. "I never like to hear the words 'kill' and 'assassin' spoken out loud, but yes, you're right," he said slowly. "There are situations where people die. And, you, my dear have become one of those unpleasant situations."

Karen just stared at him, eyes wide, lips pursed. "How much do you know?" she asked him.

"I know enough," he lied. "But, I don't concern myself with all the reasons. I am paid to do a job."

"Are you saying that you were paid to kill me?"

"Not in those words, exactly. It seems you have something that my clients want very badly. I'm supposed to get it. In fact, I hired Natalie to get it." He waited for her response.

She just looked at him in shock and tried to process what he had just said. Someone had hired Serge to find her and the tape, and then kill her. And worst of all, Natalie worked for Serge. She was in it with him. Would she really kill me? Karen had been right about Daniel, and now she was scared. Really and truly scared.

"But you hired Natalie to find me? She didn't work for you before?" Karen wanted this to be true.

"Natalie has worked for me for three years. She is one of my best people."

Karen practically fainted on hearing this. She placed her hands on the back of the couch to hold herself up. She couldn't believe her ears. Natalie, her best friend, a paid assassin? The last time Karen saw Natalie was at her brother Paul's funeral, six months ago in Kansas City. At that time, they barely spoke, and Natalie left the church right after the services, saying she had to get back to work. Three years before that, they had spent time together in Monterey when Karen had worked at the college. Natalie at that time was between jobs. She had tended bar, waited tables, and spent some time with a public relations firm. She came down to Monterey from Berkeley and stayed with Karen for six months. While they were there together they met Alessandro, and they all became good friends. Karen had an ugly break up with a man she had been dating, and then started on her quest to join the FBI. It took another six months, but Karen was finally tested and accepted, and she left Monterey for Virginia. At the same time, Natalie left Monterey and returned to Kansas City, as her mother had been diagnosed with breast cancer, the only reason she ever would have returned to her home town.

Natalie stayed with her family for four months while her mother underwent chemo and radiation, eventually surviving the cancer. While Natalie was in town, she by chance ran into Serge at a night club. They started talking, and then met again several more times, the last time with Natalie agreeing to go to work in Serge's business.

Karen thought back to the last time she had spoken to Natalie. Natalie never did tell her exactly what she was doing, she would just say that she was gainfully employed, and happy. Karen was busy, and Natalie sounded good, so Karen never pushed the matter. Now she wanted to scream at Natalie, at herself, at Serge, at everyone who had brought her to this place in her life.

"Three years," she finally moaned softly, hardly speaking. "An assassin."

She sank down on to the couch, holding her head in her hands. Serge wondered if she was going to faint. He didn't yet know what he was going to do, but he knew he did not want her unconscious. He needed to find out where the tape was. He picked up the bottle of water which was on the desk and handed it to Karen.

"Here, have a drink of water."

Karen took the bottle, but didn't take a drink. She continued to stare in disbelief at Serge.

"Quit looking at me like that,: he told her. "You must have known that people were looking for you."

"Jesus. I thought I knew. I ran because I was scared, but somewhere inside I guess I wanted to be wrong. I never internalized that someone would pay to have me killed. And now, to hear that Natalie is involved. I'm in shock."

 "Karen, I am sorry about this. But this is where we are. I need the tape, and you have it. Now, where is it?"

She looked out the window momentarily, then turned to face him as she answered, "In a safe place."

"Are you willing to die to keep it in a safe place?"

"No. I mean, I guess I never really faced the truth. I knew of persons who would want this tape very badly, but I just could not let myself believe that I could be killed over it."

"There must be something fucking awful on this tape," Serge told her, almost as a confidence, "because I have never before seen pressure like this. And from such high places."

"You could probably say that," Karen said. She could feel her old power over Serge returning. But things were critically different now. This was not high school. There was no senior ball to which he wanted to ask her, and no valedictorian speech, which she gave instead of him. This was her life, and possibly her death.

"Is there a dollar figure? What price is on my life?" She watched him for a moment, then dropped her eyes.

"If you get me the tape, we can work something out."

"Liar," she reacted. "You know that is not possible. I know what is on that tape. You don't."

"But without the tape, it's your word against…" he looked at her, "against, who? Who is on this tape?"

"Now Serge, if you really wanted to make some money, I could share with you the information on the tape. No, then you would be dead also."

"Who, Karen, who?"

She studied him, turned and looked out the window again, trying to decide what to do. At least they were talking. She was buying time. Maybe Jack would call. Oh my God, she thought, what if the President shows up.

"Serge, I have not told anyone what is on this tape, but since this may be my last conversation with another human being, I am going to tell you."

Serge just remained still and listened.

"On this tape is the President's wife in a sexual relation, a very graphic sexual relation, with the President's chief of staff, Daniel Slobe.."

"Them on tape?" he asked her in amazement. "How in the hell did that happen?"

"Well, I won't tell you that, because that would involve someone else. Just believe me when I say that if the tape goes viral, it will be the fucking end of the President, his wife, and his chief of staff. Hamilton can kiss a second term goodbye. Maybe you think it is just sex, but no, this is more than just sex, it is betrayal at the worst, and none of them will survive it."

Serge was still digesting these revelations, and just shook his head and didn't speak.

"Who paid you to find me?" she asked.

"A man I have worked for in the past." Oddly, Serge decided to confide in her also. "He is in the top echelon of the CIA. You know how dirty politics is in Washington, and brutal. Shit happens, people get involved where they shouldn't, with people they shouldn't, and sometimes they need a permanent solution. My contact is a middle man between them and me. I don't ask questions, but I can usually put scenarios together, after the fact. Does the President know about the tape?" Serge asked her.

"I don't know. But maybe he is the one who hired you?" Karen was sure it had been Daniel, but she wondered if Serge knew anything else.

Serge thought about this for a moment. Maybe it was him. He had no way of knowing who was paying Acer. He seriously doubted it was the President, though. Not directly, anyway. Now, his chief of staff, that was a different story. It could very well be him.

Serge considered all the options open to him if he had this tape. Money would be no object. He could get anything he wanted. Get out of this business for good. Seeing Karen brought back those old feelings of inferiority. He realized that he struggled each day to overcome it, and now seeing Karen, he knew that his whole business was built solely on his need to be better than her. And yet, seeing her, sensing her presence, hearing her voice, he knew, it hadn't worked. He was a failure. But, he had to finish this last assignment. Of course, she did not want to die, and, truthfully, he did not want to kill her. But, if it worked out that way, so be it.

He stood up, and for a moment, Karen thought he was going to assault her. She stiffened in readiness for an attack. But he merely turned from her and walked to the window. Then he looked back at her, unmoving, then back out the window again, staring at the lights of the city below. He was processing this information about the tape in his mind. Someone had obviously given it to Karen. Why, Serge did not know. He turned around and faced her once more, and asked, "Did this person who gave you the tape make a copy of it?"

"I don't know. When I got it, or when I first watched it, I knew I was in grave danger, and so was he. So, I took the tape and fled. Why, I can't say now. Jesus, I wish I had said to him, just go, go with this tape and don't look back."

"No one knows about this other person?"

"I'm sure by now they have made the connection. I can't tell you anymore. I don't want him involved."
"Trust me, my dear, if they know who he is, he is on someone's hit list."

Karen shuddered. She hoped Saul was deep in hiding out of the country. "I really don't know if he made a copy. He was beside himself with shock when I last saw him, scared, confused, horrified at what he had seen."

"Why did he come to you? Why not Daniel or Sarah?"

"I don't know why he didn't go to them. No, that's not true. I do know why he didn't go to Daniel. Daniel is ruthless. He probably would have been dead before he left the room if he had confronted Daniel. In fact, I'm sure it is Daniel who is behind the man you are working for. There's no doubt."

"You know Daniel well, then?"

"Well enough. He's earned his reputation."

Karen looked at her watch. Fifteen minutes to nine. It was at least an hour before the President would return to the hotel. She needed to keep Serge talking until she could figure out something to do. Likewise, Serge needed to figure out how he could get this tape from Karen. He knew that killing her now was not an option. If she were dead, how would he get the tape? Then he had an idea.

"Have you seen your parents lately?" he asked her.

"Yes," she answered warily. "But they don't have the tape. I wouldn't jeopardize them like that."

"You know,' he began slowly, "I have many people who work for me. In fact, my headquarters is in Kansas City."

Karen had not expected this. She didn't speak for a moment, but what else could she say?
"Don't hurt them. I will give you the tape. But how would I know that they are safe? They don't even know there is a tape."

"I guess you'll just have to take my word for it."

Karen laughed out loud, even surprising herself.
"Oh, Serge, this is something, isn't it? You and me, here at this moment, in this ridiculous situation. Two people fucking their brains out on tape, and I have to see it, and you have to want it." She continued to laugh, "I can't help it," she said. "I just can't believe it. I remember you from high school, smart, serious, becoming an engineer. When did everything change for you?"

"I'm still smart, and I'm still serious," he said, almost apologetically. "You know I always moved to a different beat, way different from you and your crowd. It's a rather sordid story how I got into this business. I needed money in college. Some people sold their blood or their bodies. I had a chance to join a group of businessmen looking for a younger recruit. And, I was shocked when I learned what their business was, but Karen, the money was so good. If you remember, and I'm sure you do, I was poor in high school, always on the outside looking in, dreaming of you and your fancy house and new car, and all your friends who had the same."

"Yea, I guess I knew then that you didn't have much, but you had such a future, that I didn't feel sorry for you."

"I didn't want your pity," he told her bitterly. "I just wanted to be treated as an equal."

"But you were, weren't you? I treated you like anyone else."

"You had a smile for everyone. I guess I wanted more from you."

Karen looked at him with surprising sympathy. "More? You had feelings for me?"

"Probably."

"I never knew."

"That was a very long time ago. Many lifetimes ago for me. I don't even know that person anymore. You could say that I have become new with each job I have taken."

147

"That's sick, Serge. Sick."

"Maybe, but it doesn't matter now because you are going to get me out of it. You are going to give me this tape which is going to start a new life for me." Karen gazed at Serge, but said nothing. He resumed, "First, I need to know where this tape is, and then we have to go and get it."

The "we" made her really nervous. Good God in heaven, she thought to herself, what do I do now?

"I need to go to the bathroom," she said and got up from the couch. She walked without incident into the bathroom and locked the door. She sat down on the toilet without lifting the lid. Her whole body was frozen. She knew he probably was glad she had left him alone so he could go through her things. Look up numbers in her cell phone, no doubt. Go through her suitcase. She didn't care. She needed some time to think. Jack could call at any time. Hell, the President might just knock on the door. She couldn't help but think of Natalie. Her Natalie, an assassin. Where was she now? I have no choice she told herself. I must take Serge to the tape. He doesn't have a gun, though. I'm sure he went through security. He would have shown it to me if he had one.

She hadn't used her training in martial arts for many years, but she hadn't forgotten, and she worked out at the gym every day, at least until she went on the run. Serge, too, had noticed that Karen was in top shape. Unlike her, he didn't frequent a gym. He relied on his weapons, guns, knives, poisons to subdue his victims. Karen had laughed a moment ago, but now as she stood and looked at herself in the mirror, she knew that these next few minutes would dictate the rest of her life. She had to try to take him down. What did she have to lose? She considered what she had in her suitcase to tie him up.

She flushed the toilet, then turned on the water in the sink and splashed her face with cold water, taking a towel off the rack to dry. The she opened the door and entered the room. She saw her cell phone on the desk; it had been in her purse. Serge was standing by the desk.
She was walking toward her suitcase when the cell rang. She had taken it off vibrate after her meeting with Jack. She didn't want to miss his call. She immediately ran and picked it up. Serge didn't have time to stop her, if he was going to.

"Hello," she said, and waited.

"Karen, it's Jack. Looks like we're on. My guy talked to the President. Actually, the President talked to him. Seems he is in the mood tonight.

Feeling frisky." Karen couldn't speak for a moment. "Karen?" Jack said. "Is everything all right?"

"Sure," she immediately replied, "I'm just amazed that this might come together like I planned it." She looked at Serge, who was listening intently. "When will he be here?"

"At least an hour. But he is trying to get out of the dinner as soon as he can. Guess he likes to, I don't know, guess he wants to get it on."

"Won't he be disappointed."

"Well, that's your call," Jack added dryly.

"Thanks, Jack. I'm going to change my clothes now."

"Just be ready for a knock in about an hour. And Karen, don't mess this up. Both of our asses are on the line. Sorry, wrong choice of words. You know what I mean."

"I got it, Jack. Thanks. Gotta go."

She disconnected the call while Serge looked at her waiting for an explanation.
Just for an instant, Karen eyed the window. She wondered how much force she would have to exert to throw herself through it. Falling eleven

stories might be preferable to what she was planning now.

"I guess you are wondering what that was all about," she said to Serge.

Before he had a chance to reply, she rushed toward him and kneed him hard in the groin. He doubled over, and she hit him on the back of his neck with her two hands fisted together. He fell to the floor. There she kicked him in the chest, once, then again and again. He lay there motionless. Karen grabbed her purse and ran out of the room.

When she hit him, his phone flew from his hands and rolled under the bed. When she put her hands together to strike him on the neck, she dropped her phone also. It took the same path as Serge's phone. And, now, there are two phones laying under the bed in room 1102.

Chapter Fourteen

Normally, Charles was happy to see Daniel, but this evening, he cringed inwardly when he saw him approaching. Charles was in the entry hall of the Nob Hill home of Mrs. Cora Finley, a wealthy San Francisco socialite, preparing to make his entrance. Daniel greeted Charles as normal, and Charles spoke in the usual manner also. But inside, Charles had other things on his mind, namely sex, and he didn't want Daniel messing up his night, carrying on about one of his infernal issues. Issues can wait until the morning, he told himself. And he would say the same to Daniel if he started in on anything.

"Hello, Mr. President," Daniel said loudly.

"Good evening, Daniel. I am surprised to see you here. Is anything the matter?" Charles knew he had to ask, even if he was not in the mood.

"No, everything is fine," Daniel lied. "I just thought I could make some inroads with some of the guests this evening. Perhaps set up some future fund raisers."

"Right. Good thinking," Charles answered, all the time thinking that their party had people who did just that, set up fund raisers. He wondered what was really on Daniel's mind.

"Will you be available for a little while after the dinner tonight?" Daniel asked him.

"No, Daniel, not tonight. I have plans. We can talk on the plane back to Washington."

Daniel did his best to hide his disappointment, but he wasn't going to beg for some of Charles' time, even for this crisis which was looming so large in his life. He didn't say anything, and Charles said to him, "Daniel, are you all right?"

"Yes, sir, I just have some personal things on my mind. I'm fine. We can talk tomorrow."

Daniel had a good idea what Charles was planning. He had traveled with him for the past fifteen years. He had even set up women for him in the early days. Charles would not be deterred tonight. I wonder, thought Daniel, if he would meet with me if he knew what I had to tell him. Then he remembered. Sarah was coming to Charles' hotel tonight. She might be there now. Maybe I might not be on that plane tomorrow, he thought.

"You know," Daniel said to Charles, "I've changed my mind about dinner. I'm not feeling very well after all. I think I will go the hotel and check into a room. Maybe get a good night's sleep away from Washington, D.C. for a change."

"Good Idea," Charles told him. "Take the night off. Go to the bar and have a couple of drinks. Maybe you'll get lucky. We will talk in the morning."

Just then, an older woman, dressed in Prada and pearls, took hold of Charles' arm and led him away. "Come now, Mr. President. Everyone is waiting for you to take your seat. We are all getting hungry."

Charles accompanied her obligingly and nodded at Daniel as he walked away. Daniel turned dejectedly toward the back door from which he had entered. He exited the building and walked to the street, where he hailed a taxi. Fifteen minutes later he was at the desk of the Sheraton, showing his credentials and asking for a room near the President. Daniel was given a room one floor below the President's suite, on fourteen. He took his small bag and rode the elevator to his floor. He walked to his room and opened the door with his card key. As he entered the room, he could see the city lights below. At least they gave me a room with a view, he told himself. The city lay in a sea of brightness below him, with the bay dark and looming beyond the lights. He sat down on the bed and contemplated his next move. It always came back to Sarah. He had to talk to her. He took his cell phone from his pocket and dialed her number. Four rings, no answer. He wondered if she had changed her mind and not

154

flown to San Francisco. Maybe she was drunk somewhere.

Sarah looked at her phone as it rang. Now he calls me, she said to herself. Now, that I am in my husband's hotel suite ready to confess everything. But she knew she was going to answer. She had no other choice.

"Hello," she spoke after pushing the accept call button.

"Hi, Sarah," Daniel said calmly.

"Now you return my calls. Do you know where I am?"

"I think so. San Francisco. Hotel Sheraton?"

"Where are you?"

"In the same hotel."

Sarah gasped for air and immediately eyed the mini-bar wherein stood the little bottles of courage which she needed so badly right now. "What are you doing here? You weren't scheduled to make this trip."

"Neither were you."

"I came to surprise my husband."

"I came to speak to my boss."

For a moment, they were both silent. Sarah spoke first. "Daniel, I am going to tell Charles everything. There's no other way. The tape will surface, and I would rather die than have Charles find out in that way."

Daniel felt like reducing her to shreds, but he knew he needed to tread very lightly with this conversation. "Sarah," he began, "I know how you feel. We both love Charles, but you see, we love each other, also. What we did was wrong, so wrong, but we can fix this. Meet me now, and let's come up with a plan. I have an idea which can save your marriage and my career. You are in the President's suite now?".

"Yes."

"I will walk up there now. Let the secret service know that I am coming. We can talk and decide what to do together."

"Why didn't you take my calls today?" she almost whined at him.

"I'm sorry. I am confused, too. I didn't know what to do. I know I should have talked to you earlier, but I am here now. And we can make a plan."

"All right," she said with resignation. "I will let Raul know that you are coming."

"Fine. See you in ten minutes."

He hung up, and Sarah stared into space. Her courage of the morning had somehow failed her upon hearing Daniel's voice. She walked to the mini-bar, opened the door, and removed a small bottle of gin. Removing the top, she swallowed the contents with two swallows. Immediately, she felt stronger. She took out another bottle of gin, and with it a bottle of tonic.

∞

Natalie stepped out of the Hilton into the brisk night air of San Francisco. Even though it was summer, nights in San Francisco were always cold. Natalie had asked at the front desk for directions to the Sheraton, and now she turned on Market Street and heightened her pace. Every beat of her heart was propelling her toward Karen. She knew Karen was in trouble. She arrived at the front door to the hotel and saw that a security check point had been set up in the lobby. She couldn't go in that way. She turned and walked to the alley where the back entrance to the hotel was located. That was her original plan anyway, to go in through the back, but these doors were tightly shut. She began searching in the alley for a place to hide her gun, so she could go in through the front doors and ask for a Karen Moss at the desk. She walked up and down, but she could not find any cubby or small opening to place her weapon. She felt very vulnerable without her gun, but she needed to enter the hotel. She walked to the end of the alley and turned on the street on the north side of the hotel. Then she walked back to Market Street at the front of the hotel. But there would be no hiding places in the front of the hotel because of all the lights from the street. The alley at least was dark. Maybe she had missed something. Retracing her steps in the alley, she came upon a small vent, which looked like it came from the basement of the hotel. She loosened the cover, and found that there was a small ledge inside. Checking the alley for any persons, and seeing no one, she removed her revolver from her bag and placed it on the ledge. Then she replaced the vent. Still feeling uneasy without her weapon, she started to walk to the front door of the hotel. Then, she remembered the switchblade she had put in her boot. She turned around and returned to the vent where she put the knife with the gun.

With the vent back in place, she went to the hotel entrance and walked to security. The man there asked her what her business was at the hotel, and she replied that she was with a small newspaper, and just wanted to get a feel for the atmosphere of the hotel where the President was staying.

"Okay," he told her, "come on through."

Luckily, he did not ask her for any credentials. Natalie went through the metal detector without incident and took her purse from the tray and thanked the agent.

"You're welcome," he said, all the while looking at her lithe body in the black outfit.

Natalie walked around a bit in the lobby, as if gathering information for the setting of her article. Then, she walked to one of the chairs near the desk, sat down, and pretended to look through her purse for a pad and pencil. Some other people were at the security site now, and Natalie walked to the front desk.

"Can I help you?" the young man behind the counter asked her.

"I hope so. I am looking for Karen Moss. I think she is staying here."

The blonde haired man typed the name into his keyboard and told her, "No one here by that name."

"Are you sure? Can you check again? Maybe you spelled it wrong."

The clerk scowled at her, but said, "One more time. But I'm sure I spelled it right. Last name, M-O-S-S. Right?"

"Right."

It took a moment as the clerk scanned the screen. "Not registered. No one named Moss is signed in."

"Maybe she used another name," Natalie posed.

"Maybe, but I can't stand here all night looking up supposed names of your friend."

"No, I guess you can't. Thanks anyway."

Natalie turned away from the counter and returned to one of the couches by the window. There she sat down and contemplated her feelings. She was sure Karen was here, something was going down which involved the President, and he was staying here tonight. She thought back over the instructions she had been given by Serge. Find the metal box and the tape. Find Karen. Eliminate her if necessary, but get the tape. Now, Natalie knew Karen better than anyone else on the planet. Karen would not have gone to Mexico on a whim. Or, maybe she had. Maybe it was all a decoy, a diversion. The bright, shiny metal box, something to distract the seekers of the tape. But why involve Alessandro? Alessandro. The thought of him made Natalie recoil inside. Why had Karen given the box to him? Well, she hadn't really, she had merely asked him to find it. She must have had no idea of the people who

160

were after her, how ruthless they were. Natalie knew she had to help Karen, to save Karen, in order to make up for Alessandro. She remained sitting on the couch. She couldn't move now. Her gun and knife were outside.

As she sat there, a man in a dark suit approached her and said, "Mind if I sit down?"

"No," Natalie answered, eyeing him up and down. Navy suit, gray tie, obviously a gun in the holster under the jacket.

"I couldn't help but notice you sitting here. I watched you as you came in. You are very attractive."

Natalie just stared at him and said, "So?"

"So," he began, "I might have a proposition for you."

"Now, wait a minute," she stopped him. "I am not that kind of girl. I don't know what you are thinking, but I am just looking for my friend. I thought she might be a guest here."

"Oh yea? What's her name?"

"Karen, Karen Moss."

After she said it, she knew she had said too much. For the man's face immediately registered the name. He then tried to hide it, but Natalie had seen the recognition.

"This Karen, how do you know her?"

Now Natalie was on guard. "Just someone I met a couple of nights ago at a club. Thought we might have a drink."

"I think you might want to come with me," he said to her and stood up.

"No, no, I don't," Natalie said. Then she screamed, "I just want to find Karen Moss. Karen Moss."

Everyone in the lobby looked over at her and the man with her. Jack O'Shaunessey was one of them. He quickly walked over to Natalie and the man. "What's going on, Jay? Why is she screaming?"

"He threatened me," Natalie said. "But first he propositioned me. He thought I was a hooker. I'm just looking for my friend."

"Your friend Karen?" Jack asked her.

"Well, my acquaintance, Karen."

"And you think she is here?" Jack asked.

"Yes. I think so. But they don't have her registered, so I guess I will go. She must have gone somewhere else."

"Stay here," Jack told her, motioning to the couch.

He took Jay by the arm, and led him to the other side of the lobby. He kept his eye on Natalie, but held on to Jay. Jay shook his arm from Jack's grasp and said, "She looks like a hooker to me. Came into the hotel fifteen minutes ago, and is still in the lobby. Just sitting there, waiting for who? A John, no doubt."

Jack looked at Jay and again at Natalie, now sitting up straight on the couch watching them.

"Just let it go, Jay. Let it go. If you are doing what I think you are doing, you'll have to look elsewhere tonight."

Jack was the senior agent, so Jay immediately agreed. "Fine," he said, and walked away toward the hallway where the men's restroom was located. Jack watched him for a moment, then walked quickly back to Natalie, who now was standing, looking out the window.

"Hello again," he said to her quietly.

Natalie turned to face him and said , "What the hell is going on here? Do you guys always solicit unsuspecting females?"

"Please, calm down. I need to talk to you about Karen. I am a friend of hers. How do you know her?"

"A friend? What kind of friend?" Natalie asked skeptically.

"I know her from Washington. We both work there. Tell me how you know her."

"I don't know her. We just met a few nights ago in a bar. She told me she would be staying here for a few days. That's all."

Jack knew that was a lie. Karen had just arrived in San Francisco this morning. He knew what kind of people might be after Karen and the tape, and he wondered if this dark haired woman was one of them.

"Look," Natalie said to him, "I just found her attractive, that's all. I wanted to get to know her better. It just didn't work out. She's not here, and I will go."

Now, Jack and Natalie both knew that the other one was hiding something. Natalie knew that when she screamed Karen's name and Jack walked over that he must have information about

Karen, and Jack knew that Natalie must know something about Karen and the tape also, or why would she be screaming her name and looking for her in this hotel. He didn't want Natalie to leave, but he didn't know how he could keep her here. He didn't want to tell her too much if she was one of the group, undoubtedly hired by Daniel, to find Karen and the tape.

"Just a minute," he said to her, and pulled back his jacket, exposing his revolver in the holster over his shoulder. "How do I know you are not a threat to the President?"

Natalie backed away two steps. She looked for a chair, and sat down, all the time watching Agent O'Shaunessey. Obviously, he knew something, but she didn't know whose side he was on either. While O'Shaunessey and Natalie were searching their minds for the next thing to say, Jay Aldred stood in the hallway watching the scene unfold before him. He removed the cell phone from his jacket and dialed a number.

Chapter Fifteen

In his hotel room, Daniel disconnected the call to Sarah. Then he went to his suitcase and removed a small length of rope. He also removed a small bottle of sleeping pills, 20 mg Ambien capsules prescribed by his doctor. He poured the pills onto the bed, opening six of them and pouring the contents back into the bottle. Then he placed the bottle in his inside jacket pocket. He tossed the remainder of the capsules into his suitcase. The rope he coiled and put in the front pocket of his slacks. He also took his wool scarf he had worn from Washington and folded it and placed in his outer jacket pocket. He stood there for a moment and contemplated what he was planning. Was he capable of killing Sarah? If his plan worked, it would be easy. He would make her a couple of drinks that he laced with the Ambien. She would be drugged with alcohol and sleeping pills, then he would use the rope to strangle her. Or, he could use the scarf to suffocate her.

He left his room and walked to the elevator at the end of the hall. He rode up one flight to the floor of the President's suite. As the elevator door opened, he was met by three agents standing watch. He greeted them with a smile. "I am going in to have a chat with the first lady. We are working on a surprise for the President."

"Sure," one of the men said, and all three stepped away from the door to the suite. "Just let us know if you need anything," the agent named Raul said.

"Thanks," Daniel replied while knocking on the door. In a moment, the door opened, and Sarah appeared, holding on to the handle, as if for support. "Come in, Daniel," she slurred.

Daniel looked back one last time at the agent who had spoken and said "Later."

Raul just nodded and resumed his post at the door. Inside, Daniel saw that Sarah was holding a drink. Seeing this, Daniel felt a bit of confidence, but made no comment. He walked over to a chair and sat down, feeling for the bottle of pills in his pocket. Sarah noticed the motion, but said nothing.

For a moment, they just stared at each other. Finally, Daniel spoke. "Sarah, my love," he began. At "my love" Sarah walked also to a chair and sat down facing him. "Seeing you almost makes it all worthwhile. But we have got to come up with a plan to take us out of this mess we have created. Do you agree?"

"Of course. But, really, what can we do? We don't have the tape. Saul is gone, God only knows where, and who knows how many copies of the tape he made before he left. And, Karen, also unknown whereabouts, she must have a copy also. We are doomed."

Daniel replied, "I have people who are looking for Saul and Karen. They will find them and retrieve the tape or tapes. Trust me, I have my best people working on this."

Sarah didn't doubt that Daniel had hired the best people, best meaning the most ruthless and unprincipled people on the planet. In this realm, Daniel was an expert. Sarah didn't often admit it, but much of Charles' success was because of Daniel's "people". Elections won by intimidation, bills passed by threats. Daniels's investigations into the private lives of legislators always turned up something tawdry and useful.

"What is your plan, Daniel?" she asked him. She took a long drink from her gin and tonic, eyeing the glass to see how much was left. Daniel, too, looked at the contents of the glass.

"Well, I've been thinking. We could tell Charles that we had just the one incident together, that we had resisted our feelings for a long time, but this day, well something happened between us, and we could no longer hold back. Afterward, we told each other that this would never happen again, that we were so ashamed and sorry for what we had done. All would have been well, except for the tape, which you had forgotten was running, and which I knew nothing about."

"And you think he will believe that?"

"I don't know.   Maybe not, but he would rather believe a lie than hear the truth.   That we had been fucking our brains out for three years, right under his nose."

"Jesus, Jesus Christ," Sarah moaned.   "Is that what we did?"

"You know exactly what we did, Sarah.   Get your head out of the fucking sand, no, out of the fucking bottle, for just one minute and look at us. Yes, we betrayed the President of the United States.   How do you feel about that?"

"He's my husband first, then he's the President. That's no one seems to understand.   My husband first, then the fucking leader of the free world.   God, I am so sick of being the President's wife.   Just stand here, Sarah, just smile, just have the kids show up and look handsome anytime we ask you.   Jesus Christ, we are humans, just people like everyone else in the world.   I can't take the scrutiny anymore."   She drained the contents of the glass and rose to get a refill.

Daniel quickly stood and took the glass from her hand.   "Let me," he said.   Sarah sat back down and watched as he walked over to the bar and removed the bottle of gin from the shelf.

"I see you ordered a bottle of gin," he said to her. He poured the glass half full, then opened the small refrigerator under the bar.

"Sarah, will you get some more ice from the kitchen?" he asked her. "This ice maker doesn't seem to be working." She eyed him strangely, but stood up and walked toward the kitchen at the back of the suite. She paused once inside the doorway and looked back. She saw Daniel pour something from a pill bottle into the glass. He then put the small container back into his pocket. She said nothing, but went to the cabinet and removed a glass, filled it with ice from the refrigerator door, and returned to Daniel, who was now holding the glass with gin and tonic, but no ice. She handed him the ice and said, "I need something from my room. I will be right back."

She walked into her bedroom and picked up her purse which was lying on the bed. She opened the inside zippered pocket and removed a small gun, a derringer, two shots. She held the gun in her left hand, and kept it behind her back. She then returned to the chair where she had been sitting. Daniel brought her the drink he had made. "I really wish you weren't drinking now," he sighed as he handed it to her.

"I'll bet," she answered as she took the drink with her right hand, her left hand cradling the gun behind her. She set the drink on the table by the chair and sat down. Her heart was racing, and her brain was scrambling for a reason not to use the gun. But no reason came, only rage. She watched him sit down, then she began.

"So you think we tell Charles that we had a one-time fling, made the biggest mistake of our lives, and he will believe it? You're out of your mind. No, wrong, you are just Daniel, making up stories and alibis, not meaning anything you say. Charles won't believe that story. He has eyes. He has seen us look at each other for these past fifteen years. He's had affairs, I know that. And I don't think he would really care if you and I had an affair, if we fucked like rabbits for years. But what he will care about is his reputation. If the tape goes public, his career is over. Hell, his life will be over. All of our lives will be over. So, Daniel, my lover, my confidante, is that why you just laced my drink with poison? You know my life is over anyway, and how convenient if I just went away. Suicide, and you found me. Oh, you would put the right spin on it. Well, bastard, I won't go down that way."

She stood up and pointed the gun at Daniel. "I think I will take you down first."

Daniel looked at the gun in horror. "Sarah, no," he yelled.

Then she pulled the trigger, put a bullet right into his chest, then another into his head. She stood there and watched as he slumped in the chair. Then she dropped the gun. Immediately, the door was thrown open and Raul and two other agents ran in.

"Are you all right?" Raul asked her and looked at Daniel bleeding in the chair and Sarah standing in a daze before him.

"No, Raul, I'm not all right. And neither is he."

She picked up the glass and handed it to him. "Keep this," she said. "He tried to poison me."

She watched as Raul took the glass and carefully set it on the table between the two chairs.

He then knelt down and felt Daniel's neck for a pulse. Nothing. He stood and instructed the other agents. "Just wait outside and secure the area. Don't let anyone in here until Jack arrives. I am calling him now."

The two men surveyed the scene before them, but obeyed Raul and left the suite, closing the door solidly behind them. The image of Sarah Hamilton standing in front of a blood-soaked Daniel Slobe, now mangled in the chair, was lodged in their brains forever. When they had gone, Raul, eyeing the gun on the floor, said to Sarah, "Is this the gun you fired?"

"Yes," she answered, and practically fell into the chair behind her. "Yes, that is my gun. He was trying to kill me."

Jack's phone rang, and he pulled it from his pocket. "O-Shaunessey," he said.

"Jack. Come to the President's suite now. We have a catastrophe."

"What happened?"

"Daniel Slobe is dead. I'm here now with Sarah Hamilton. Looks like she shot him."

Jack immediately turned toward the elevators, then said to Natalie, "I have an emergency."
Then he ran and pushed the "up" button, waiting impatiently for the car to arrive. It was taking too long, so he ran to the stairwell, but remembering it was fourteen floors, he turned back to the elevator. The doors mercifully opened, and he entered and pushed "Penthouse Suite". As the doors closed, blocking out his image, both Natalie, in the lobby, and Jay, from a vantage point in the corridor, watched in awe, wondering what had just happened.

Chapter Sixteen

As the elevator car with Jack in it ascended the shaft, the adjacent car descended, and opened its doors onto the lobby. As the metal doors opened, Karen stepped quickly from the car and hurried to the front door of the hotel. Natalie watched in amazement as her friend exited the building. She jumped up and followed immediately. Jay, still in the corridor, now stepped into the main lobby, and again dialed the number which connected him to Acer. What the hell should he do now?

Natalie got outside the hotel and looked up and down the street, but didn't see Karen. She noticed several bars on the street, and figured that Karen had gone into one of them. But before looking for Karen, she had to retrieve her weapons. She ran into the alley and lifted the grate and took out her gun and knife. Putting the knife in her boot and the gun in her bag, she hurried to the street and looked again, hoping to see Karen. No sign. Turning right, she walked toward a sign that read "Monk's". She entered the small bar and looked around. Just a few men sitting at the bar, and another two at a table watching a baseball game.

"Have you seen a blond, dressed in red, come in here just a minute ago?" she asked the tall and bearded bartender. "Nope," he answered.

Natalie hurried out and noticed another bar on the opposite side of the street. The sign outside was flashing "Jack's Place." She ran across the street, dodging traffic, and went into the bar. This place was bigger and nicer, with lighted votive candles on each table. There was a wooden bar with about ten bar stools, behind which was a woman, replacing glasses in the holder above the rows of liquor. Natalie approached the woman, and said, "Excuse me, but have you seen a blonde woman, in a red dress, come in here?"

The woman motioned to the back corridor without speaking. Natalie at once walked that direction and found the women's restroom in the corridor. She pushed open the door, but saw no one. The outer room was empty. She went into the next room with two stalls and looked under the doors, again no one. She came back out and was about to go back to the bartender, when she looked down to the end of the hall and saw Karen, speaking on a pay phone. Natalie looked for an exit door at the end of the hall and saw none. She stood where she was and waited as Karen finished her conversation. She tried to hear what was said, but the music from the bar was very loud, and Karen was speaking in low tones, so Natalie could not make out anything. She braced herself for the surprise which Karen would have when she saw her. In another minute, which seemed to Natalie like an hour, Karen hung up and turned around.

Upon seeing her friend, Karen stood motionless in her tracks. She looked around for a place to run, but saw no escape. Her next instinct was to attack Natalie and beat her senseless, but something in Natalie's face held her back. Natalie readied herself for Karen's attempt to run around her, but then relaxed when she saw that Karen was not moving.

"Christ, Natalie," Karen finally said. "Do you want to kill me too?"

"No, Karen, no. I want to help you. We need to get out of sight."

"Nat," Karen said, using her old nickname, "according to Serge, who I just left unconscious on my hotel room floor, you work for him and were hired to kill me."

"Partly true. But, I'm not going to kill you, never was. I want to help you, believe me. We need to get out of here. I have a room at the Hilton, and we will be safe there. But we need to move now. Serge is probably awake now and looking for you."

Karen studied her friend. She wanted desperately to believe her, to find out that Natalie was not a paid assassin hunting her down. Natalie took Karen's arm, and together they walked to the front door of the bar. Natalie opened the door and scanned the street scene. "I don't see anything. Let's get a cab."

They walked into the street, and Natalie hailed a cab. They got in and Natalie instructed the driver to the Hilton. Karen wanted desperately to relax, but she would not let down her guard. She looked over at Natalie as the cab started down the street. Yet neither woman said anything.

Natalie spoke first. "You must be in some pretty deep shit," she said.

"You think?" Karen said and smiled.

"I have worked for Serge for three years, and I have never seen anything like this."

"So, it's true. Serge told me you worked for him, but I just couldn't believe it." She looked full force into Natalie's eyes.

Natalie looked down. "I'm not proud of what I've become. But, you know, I've never been very proud of who I was. Life was different for me, Karen. I wasn't the darling of everyone around me. I was strange, never did fit in. Why start now?"

Karen wanted to scream at her, "You're a murderer!" Instead, not speaking, she held up her hand and pointed to the driver. They rode in silence for the five minutes it took to get to the hotel.   Karen got out first, and resisted the temptation to just run down the street, just run and run, never stopping until this whole mess went away.   But, she stood there and waited while Natalie paid the driver and got out of the cab. Karen followed Natalie into the hotel where they took the elevator up to the fifth floor and went to Natalie's room.   Once inside, both studied the surroundings for signs of intrusion. Seeing that nothing looked out of place, Karen sat down on the bed, and Natalie went to the mini-bar and pulled out two bottles of beer. She opened both and handed one to Karen.   Then she pulled the desk chair up to the bed and sat facing her friend.

Karen spoke first.   "How did you know where to find me?"

"I just finally put it all together. Serge sent me to Mexico to find you and a tape, a politically sensitive tape, something that if it went public would rock the country. And yes, he wanted me to kill you." Karen grimaced but said nothing.

"I went to Zihuatanejo and located Alessandro, because I knew he was there, and I thought you would go to him if you were there. He told me he had seen you a few days earlier. I was with him when he found the jeweled box you dropped in the ocean. That was a miracle. I couldn't tell him what I was really doing, and he was very

178

protective of the box once he had found it. He said you told him to keep it in a safe place and contact you once he found it. I went looking for the box after he had brought it to shore. I knew he must have hid it somewhere."

"Did you get the box?"

"No, I didn't find it."

"And Alessandro? Is he all right?"

Natalie dreaded this question and wanted to die right then, but she answered her friend. "He's dead. I shot him."

Karen put her hand to her mouth and moaned loudly, "Oh God. God, Alessandro. What have I done?"

Hatred for herself and Natalie now boiled in her blood. She had asked Alessandro to find the box, hadn't she? She had dropped it into the bay hoping to throw anyone searching for the tape off the scent. Now Alessandro was dead. And she was sitting across from his murderer.

"I just don't know where to begin to say I'm sorry for Alessandro," Natalie finally spoke. "I only know that I am not the same woman that went down to Mexico two days ago. I just don't want you to be hurt. When Serge asked me if I could do this assignment, I of course said yes. But I knew I would never hurt you. What a fucking idiot he is, to believe me when I said I could kill you, my soul mate, my best friend, the one person I always felt understood me and loved me for who I was. But trust me, if there was a contract out on your life, I wanted it. And look, I've saved you."

"Nat," Karen began, "I'm telling you, this is the most bizarre and surreal happening in my existence. I can't tell you what my life has been like since I got that tape. Being here with you, seeing Serge this afternoon, learning that you both kill people for a living. Jesus, God, I am in the twilight zone." She took a long drink from the bottle, and continued. "Serge was looking for you today. I was registered under your name."

"My name?"

"Why not? I didn't think you would be in San Francisco."

"He must have lit up when he saw you. He was under severe pressure to find you and the tape."

"He threatened to kill my parents if I didn't give it to him."

"He'd do it, too. Did you give it to him?"

"No, I don't have it with me. When he was in my hotel room, I got an opportunity, and I kneed him in the groin and then whacked him in the back of the head. I left him lying on the hotel room floor."

"Was he dead?"

"No, I don't think so. I just knocked him out. Than I ran."

"It's been twenty minutes. He might be awake now."

"Oh my God," Karen said as she remembered her rendezvous with the President. "I've got someone coming to my hotel room. He might find Serge there."

"Someone? Who?"

"Someone who was going to help me get out of this mess."

"Who is it?" Natalie pressed her. "Someone you trust?"

"No, no, I'm not sure, I mean, I don't know who to trust. But I had to try to stop all this madness. I wish to God I hadn't run when I first got the tape. If I had just gone to certain people then, Alessandro would still be alive."

"Please, I can't talk about Alessandro. My demons are taking me over. Will you tell me what is on that tape?"

"No. I need to make a call." She reached for her purse, then remembered that Serge had taken her cell phone after she spoke to Jack. "Serge has my phone," she told Natalie. He took it in the hotel room. I forgot to get it when I ran out. I wish I would have taken his phone. He'll find us, I know."

"How will he know where to find us? We haven't called each other. You didn't call him from this room. Did you make any calls?"

"No, none."

"So, we're safe. How would he find us here?"

∞

As Natalie thought about the possibility that Serge could find them, Serge was slowly sitting up and rubbing the back of his head. He heard a phone ringing and looked around the room. No Karen, and the phone kept ringing. He reached into his pocket and his phone was gone. Then he remembered that he was holding his phone when Karen attacked him. He stood up slowly and looked around the room and listened, but the ringing had stopped. Then it started again. He realized it was coming from under the bed.

He gingerly kneeled down and raised the bedspread. There under the bed, lay two phones. He reached under and grabbed the one that was ringing.

"Hello," he said anxiously. It was Acer, on his phone. Acer explained to Serge what had just happened in the lobby. His operative, Jay, had seen both Karen and Natalie, less than an hour ago. Natalie had been talking to the senior agent in charge of the Presidential security assignment, and he sent Jay away so they could talk in private. Jay continued to watch them, and in a couple of minutes, Jack answered a call on his cell, and ran furiously to the elevator, then the stairs, then back to the elevator and got in and disappeared. Then, as he was going up, a car came down in to the lobby, and Karen got off and ran out of the hotel. Natalie had run after her.

Serge's mind was spinning. Karen and Natalie in the same hotel, both in San Francisco, but now together and out of his reach. Acer continued. He had traced Natalie to the Hilton. Serge continued to rub his head, and formulated a plan. He told Acer that he would take care of the situation, and Acer had replied that it was all on him now, that they needed the tape, and don't eliminate either one of them if they can lead them to the tape. Serge agreed openly, but inwardly, he knew that it might not be possible. He left the room, and walked to the stairwell, where he ran down the stairs and then through the lobby and out of the hotel. He found a cab in front and got in.

"Hilton Hotel," he told the driver.

"I just went there," the driver told him.

"Two women?" Serge asked.

"How did you know?"

"Just a hunch," Serge answered, not believing his luck for the second time that day.

Arriving at the Hilton, Serge paid the driver, and entered into the lobby. There was a door to the left which led to the stairs. Serge went there and retrieved a bag which was sitting inside the door.

∞

At the dinner, blithely unaware of what had transpired this evening at his hotel, Charles Hamilton chatted with his hostess. As he spoke to her, an agent tapped him on the shoulder and told him that there was an important call for him. With apologies, he excused himself and followed the agent to the security location in the entry of the home. He took the cell phone handed to him from an agent and heard Jack O'Shaunessey's voice.

"Mr. President, we've had a tragedy. Daniel has been shot. He's in your suite at the hotel. We need you to come here immediately."

"Shot?" Charles could not believe what he was hearing. "Is he all right?"

"No, sir. He's dead."

"Holy Jesus! What happened?"

"It looks like it might have been Sarah."

Charles practically fell over, but caught his breath, and replied, "Sarah? My wife is there?"

"Yes, sir. She's here, in your suite. Just get here as fast as you can. I don't know how it happened or what happened, but we need your help."

"Don't call anyone else until I get there. Just leave things as they are. Secure the room, and don't let anyone in. I'm on my way. Jack, I'm trusting you with this."

"I'll take care of everything, sir. Just get here quick."

In thirty minutes, the President entered the penthouse suite at the Sheraton. There he found Sarah, sitting on a couch in the small parlor, sipping on a glass of wine. He looked at

185

her and didn't speak, but followed Jack into the suite through the bedroom to the small office at the back where he found his chief of staff lying in a pool of blood on the floor. On the table were an unfinished drink and a small revolver. Charles took a deep breath, and asked Jack, "What happened here?"

Jack explained how the agents outside in the hall had heard gunshots and then ran into the suite and to the back to find Sarah standing in front of Daniel's body. The gun was on the floor in front of Sarah. Daniel was shot in the chest and the head, and he had no pulse when the men arrived. Raul called Jack who came up to the suite immediately and secured the area. Then he called Charles.

"Have you spoken to Sarah?" Charles asked Jack.

"Only to ask her if she was all right."

"And she didn't say anything?"

"She told Raul that Daniel had tried to poison her." He pointed to the drink on the table. "She said the poison was in that glass."

Charles took a handkerchief from his pocket and picked up the glass and took it to the counter. The he lifted the gun and put it in his pocket.

186

"I am going to talk to Sarah. Be sure no one touches that glass. We will need it and the contents."

"What about him?" Jack asked, looking at the corpse.

Charles looked at Daniels's lifeless body also, and then said without emotion, "I just need ten minutes with Sarah, then we will call the authorities."

He walked into the other room where Sarah was sitting and sat down beside her on the couch. She seemed to be in a trance.

"Sarah, what happened here?" he gingerly asked her, not knowing how much she had been drinking.

Sarah looked up at him and said sadly, "What happened here started years ago. I just ended it."

"Sarah," Charles said this time with more resolve, "Daniel is dead. He has been shot. Did you do it?"

"We need to talk," she answered. "I need to talk to you alone. Can you find a place where we can talk alone, just you and me, no secret service, just us. I need to talk to you."

187

Charles looked back toward the room where Daniel lay dead on the floor. He knew they had to call the police. It had already been too long. He rose from the couch and called to Jack. Jack came into the room from the back, and Charles said to him, "Jack, Sarah and I need to be alone for a while. Can you find us a room where we can talk?"

Jack looked back to the place where lay Daniel's body, and Charles said, "As soon as we return, you can call the police. I need to speak to Sarah alone before they see her."

Jack thought for a moment, then he remembered that Karen was in room 1102. "I think I have a place you can go." He took out his phone and dialed Karen's cell. There was no answer. She wouldn't have left, he thought. He went to the entry of the suite, opened the door and called Raul. He told him to take the President and the First Lady to room 1102. "Just knock on the door, and leave them alone in there, then come back here. If someone is in the room, bring her up here to me."

Raul, the President, and the First Lady then left the suite and took the stairs down to eleven and went down the hall to room 1101. Walking to the room, they found that the door was partially open. Raul knocked and then pushed the door open wide. "Wait here," he told the President.

"Is anybody here?" he said and looked inside. When there was no answer, he went into the room and looked into the bathroom and the closet. Seeing that the room was empty, he brought Charles and Sarah in. Then he left, closing the door behind him.

Sarah, barely able to stand, sat down in the chair by the window. Charles went to the mini-bar and removed a small bottle of vodka. He poured the contents into a glass and pulled the desk chair up in front of his wife.

"Now, we are alone. Tell me what happened."

Chapter Seventeen

Natalie and Karen were drinking their second beer when the phone rang. Both of them just stared at the blaring instrument on the desk.

"It's him. I know it is," Karen said.

Natalie just looked between her and the phone, deciding if she should answer or not.

"He's here Natalie. I know it. I feel it."

Still, Natalie watched the phone, as if to make it go away by sheer will. But it keeps on ringing. "He knows we are here, too," Natalie says finally, and picks up the phone.

"Hello," Serge says as the ringing stops and someone finally answers. "Natalie, is that you?"

"I'm here," Natalie responds soberly. "Hold on."

She places her hand over the mouth piece and motions to Karen to leave. "Get out now," she whispers and points toward the door. "Now, quickly, before he gets up here."

"What about you?" Karen asks her.

"I'll be fine. I want you gone. Don't take the stairs. Use the freight elevator at the end of the corridor through the double doors."

Karen immediately grabs her purse and heads for the door. She looks back at Natalie, then runs back to her and they embrace. They pull apart, just staring at one another, neither knowing just what to say. Natalie speaks first, "Just go now. I'll find you."

Karen nods, walks to the door, opens it and enters the hallway. She runs down the corridor toward the double doors, flinging them open and finding the freight elevator where she pushes the down button.

When she had gone, Natalie removed her hand from the phone, and said, "Are you still there?"

Her heart skipped a beat when Serge didn't answer right away. "Yes," he said. "What room are you in?"

"612," Natalie told him. She knew it was useless to lie. He would find out anyway.

"Don't leave. And keep Karen there also."

It never ceased to amaze Natalie how Serge knew everything. She hung up the phone and went to her purse lying on the bed, where she took out her revolver and checked to be sure it was loaded and ready to fire. Then she went to her suitcase on the stand in the closet and removed yet another gun, an automatic. It, too, was loaded. Then she walked to the window and looked out at the lights of San Francisco. It was stunning. For a moment she let herself drift into the pattern of the lights. She felt the movement of the traffic on the Golden Gate Bridge. She hesitated, standing with two loaded guns in her hands, then she placed both guns on the desk, opened the door ajar, and waited.

It took two minutes for Serge to climb the stairs to six and walk to number 612. He slowly pushed open the door into the room and looked around. Seeing Natalie, he stepped in, and looked further for Karen. Then he pushed the door closed, pulling the security latch into the locked position.

"Where is she?" he asked.

"Gone, you just missed her."

"Are you crazy? Just missed her?" Serge was becoming livid. "She was our target. Why did you let her leave?"

"Why did you follow me to San Francisco?"

"Because you fucked up in Mexico. You killed the one person down there who had the tape. Did you find the tape before you left?" he questioned her.

"Maybe."

"Maybe? Quit playing games, Natalie. You fuck up in Mexico, and now you have Karen, and then you let her go."

"Serge," Natalie said with superiority, "did you really think I would kill my best friend? Just like in high school, you don't understand what it means to have a friend. You never had any."

Serge watched her, and said, with confusion, "You mean this has all been a ruse? You went to Mexico to help Karen. But, you killed a man, a friend."

 "I've lived a thousand lifetimes since I shot Alessandro," Natalie responded. "When I left him lying on that floor, I left some of myself with him. I killed us both. I knew then that you would be after me. How did you find me?"

"I talked to airport security. They told me you had flown to San Francisco. When I learned that the President was coming here, it figured that Karen would be here too. I went to the President's hotel, thinking that you might be there, also looking for Karen. I guess you figured out that this case revolves around the President."

"I put that much together," Natalie told him.

"When I went to the room," Serge continued, "that I thought was yours, there was Karen. I couldn't believe my luck."

"Then she overpowered you," Natalie said with scorn.

"She did. She's strong, and she fucking kicked me in the nuts. She knocked me out. I wasn't ready for that."

"Did you find out about the tape, what was on it?" Natalie asked him.

"Not exactly," he lied. "Just something horrific that the people in Washington want to keep secret at all costs. I can only assume it involves the President. Did Karen tell you where the tape is?"

Natalie was quiet for moment, thinking of her limited options. Then, she spoke, "Serge, you want the tape, I know. It must be worth millions. If I take you to it, will you let me live?"

"Of course. I just want to secure the tape and collect my money."

"What about Karen? Will she be safe?"

"She knows what is on that tape, and what if she made a copy? No, I don't think she can ever be safe again in this country."

Natalie listened to his words, and wondered with regret where life had taken them, and why had they wound up in this horrible place.

"The tape is here," she said slowly. "Karen had it with her all the time."

Serge looked at Natalie with surprise. "And she didn't take it now?"

"She was going to leave it on the roof. We can go up there now and get it."

Serge thought for a moment and knew that this sounded ridiculous, that Karen would never part with the tape, but he had to find out. He pulled his gun from his pocket and pointed it at Natalie. "Let's go there now. Are those your only weapons?" he asked, looking at the two guns on the desk.

"Just those," Natalie answered, and started walking towards the door. She stopped and picked up her purse, but Serge took it from her, saying, "I'll carry this."

She just looked back at him and went into the hallway, turning toward the stairs. They walked up the stairs in silence to the last landing before the roof. They reached a door reading "Roof Access".

"Open the door," Serge told Natalie.

Natalie turned the handle, but the door was locked.

"And you say she left the tape up here?"

"That's what she told me. I stayed in the room."

"Move over," he instructed her, then he shot a cartridge into the lock and pulled the door open. "You first," he told her.

Natalie walked out onto the roof, feeling the cold wind on her face. It was very dark.

"She told me she left it near an access panel on the west side."

Serge looked around for a moment, trying to get his bearings, then looked toward the Golden Gate Bridge in the distance. "This way," he pointed and Natalie walked toward the view of the bridge. When she reached the side, she stopped and turned around, then spoke slowly to Serge.

"This is the end for me," she said, as she stepped onto the upper ledge of the roof and looked down at the street below. "I'm finished. See those lights down there, the twinkling, starry lights. Aren't they amazing?"

"Natalie, come down from there," he said, keeping his distance, in case she might grab him and take him with her. "Come down. We will find the tape, collect the money and then quit this awful business. I can give you enough money to start a new life."

"I am starting a new life," she told him. "Just not on this side of the conundrum. I lied. Karen doesn't have the tape. I don't know where it is. She wouldn't tell me."

She then reached down into her boot and pulled out her knife, and as she stood up, Serge sent a bullet into her chest, whirling her from the roof, her body sailing into the lights, dropping from this earth into the abyss of the beyond. Serge watched for a shocked instant, then turned and fled the roof.

Chapter Eighteen

In the hotel room, Sarah looked at her husband tragically and began to speak. "Charles, Daniel and I have been having an affair. It's been going on now for three years. But actually, it started long ago, we just never acted on our feelings. But for the last three years we have been lovers." Charles just looked at her and said nothing.

"In the last few months, something was changing between us, and I believe we were ready to call it off, but two weeks ago something terrible happened. I hired someone to place a device in the smoke alarm in Carrie's room so I could watch her to see if she was using drugs. This tape was our undoing." She hesitated, not wanting to confess that she and Daniel had been in their daughter's bed to make love.

"Go on," Charles told her. "You were ready to call it off."

"Well, we arranged to meet one afternoon in Carrie's room," she continued, as Charles grimaced, unable to hide his feelings, which he desperately wanted to keep inside. "We met there and made love, and it was all recorded on tape."

"You and Daniel making love and on tape?" Charles erupted. "But you knew it was there, right?"

"Yes, yes, I did know. But I had been drinking, more heavily that I thought, I guess, and I didn't realize that the tape was running that afternoon. When I took the card, it was a small card for recording, to be checked, it was discovered that Daniel and I were on it."

"Wait. Sarah, you had the tape installed. How could you not know it was recording?"

"Like I said, I had been drinking a lot. I just forgot."

As the weight of this confession began to sink in, Charles again asked her, "But, you have the tape, the card, now? Tell me you have the tape now."

"I have a DVD, a copy, but there is an original, on a smaller card that wouldn't play in my machine. Oh, God, Charles, if that recording falls into the wrong hands or is made public. I just can't tell you how frantic I have been. And Daniel wouldn't even talk to me. He told me he would handle it."

"Just let me get this straight," he strained. "There was a card in the smoke alarm in Carrie's room, and it has a fucking session of you and

Daniel on it. And, you took the tape, the card, out of the smoke alarm, and then did what with it?"

"It would not fit in my computer, so I gave it to Saul Abrams, the person who installed it in the first place, a person I could trust, and asked him to put it on a DVD which I could watch."

"And you never got the original back?"

"No, I didn't. Oh, God, I know how stupid I was, and now I don't know why I started this whole recording thing in the first place. I was worried about Carrie, and you were never around."

"Stop. Jesus Christ, just stop," Charles rebuked her. "It's too late for recriminations against me and our marriage and my lack of concern for the children and you. You were taking care of yourself, Daniel and booze, your constant companions." He looked heartlessly at her. She stared at the floor, then took the glass of vodka from him and began to drink.

"Why did you shoot Daniel? Does he have the tape?"

"No, he had people looking for Karen Moss and Saul, but no luck. I don't know where the tape is now. For all I know, Saul took the only copy out of the country or threw it in the Potomac."

"Karen Moss? What does she have to do with it? Didn't she work in the residence for a while?"

"Yes. She also worked with Saul. Daniel thinks she has a copy of the tape."

"But you aren't sure what happened. No one has contacted me about blackmail. Has anyone threatened you?"

"No," she said. "I wish they had. Then at least I would have a lead as to where I could find the tape."

Charles looked at his watch. Ten minutes had passed. They had to return upstairs. In all his years in politics, nothing like this had ever happened. He could always take any problem in stride and fix it.   Right now, his brain was scrambling for a solution, Daniel dead, shot by Sarah, a tape with his wife and chief of staff screwing in his daughter's room, and two people, Saul Abrahms and Karen Moss, who might have this tape. What was he to do now?

He stood up and took the glass from Sarah. "Stand up," he told her.   "We need to call the police. You say Daniel tried to kill you. How?"

"He put poison in my drink. I saw him."

Charles pondered this. He had a hundred more questions for Sarah, but they would have to wait until another time. He hoped there would be another time. "Sarah, I am sorry, sorry for everything I have ever done to you or not done for you. I know this is partly my fault. We will get through this."

As he spoke these words, a phone rang. Charles and Sarah looked around the room, and after the fifth ring, Charles reached under the bed, pulled out a cell phone and answered. "Hello?"

"Mr. President?" Jack said.

"Jack?"

"It's me. Are you ready to come back upstairs?"

"We are. Whose phone is this? Who are you calling?"

"I will explain when you get here. Bring the phone with you. Shall we call the police now?"

"Call the Mayor, the Police Commissioner, and the Chief of Police. Tell them it is an emergency and to come to my suite at the hotel immediately."

Chapter Nineteen

Karen rode the freight elevator in abject fear, and when the doors opened on the ground floor, she peeked out cautiously, scanning the empty corridor. To her right was a set of double doors. She ran to them and pushed her way into the back of the kitchen. The smell of food and the sounds of the staff bombarded her. She rushed between the counters and cabinets in search of an exit. Seeing windows and then a door, she ran and threw herself outside. The doors slammed behind her, and for a moment she breathed in the cold night air.

Now what, she asked herself. She thought about helping Natalie, but Natalie and Serge were partners. She couldn't go back there. Natalie would take care of herself. In fact, Serge might be dead at this very minute. She couldn't go back into the hotel. She thought about her meeting with the President. Maybe it wasn't too late. Maybe he hadn't shown up yet. She began running to the street and turned toward the Sheraton. She just kept running, she would not get in a cab until she was a far distance from this hotel. She caught a cab after seven blocks, and in ten minutes more she stepped from the cab and entered the security booth at the Sheraton. There weren't many agents in the lobby. The President must already be upstairs, she thought. She got on the elevator and rode to five, then took the stairs to eleven and walked to room

1102. The door was closed and locked. She retrieved her key and opened the door. Walking in, she noticed that a chair had been pulled up and was facing the couch by the window. Serge was gone. Maybe Hamilton did show up, she thought. The she started looking for her phone. She looked in the bathroom, on the desk and counters, even under the bed. No phone. Serge has it, she concluded.

Serge. God, I hope Natalie shot him, and he is laying in a pool of his own blood on that hotel room floor, but somehow, she didn't believe that. She knew somewhere deep inside that Natalie was the one who was gone. She felt trapped in the room, but at the same time, where was she going to go? Maybe she had come to the end of the line with this espionage and running around the country.

"I wanted to speak to the President, and I shall keep trying," she said aloud. She picked up the hotel phone and dialed Jack's number. He answered immediately. "Jack, it's me, Karen."

"Karen, where are you?"

There was something unnatural in his voice, and Karen was immediately on edge. "Where are you?" she questioned in response.

"I'm in the President's suite, upstairs. We came to your room, and you weren't there."

Now, Karen heard in particular the "we", "we" came to your room. There was to be no "we", just the President in all is horny glory. Something is not right, she reasoned.

"Are you close by? We can come and get you," Jack told her.

There he goes again with that "we". "No, I'm not close. Something happened, and I had to leave the room in a hurry."

"It must have been a real hurry," he said. "We found your cell phone under the bed."

"Was the President in my room?" she asked Jack. "Did he take my phone?"

"It's complicated," Jack said. "Look, it's imperative that you come and talk to us right away. Just tell me where you are, and we can come and get you. You'll be safe with us."

A feeling of dread ran from Karen's head to her ankles, and she suddenly realized that in any minute they could trace her to the phone in the room. "Gotta go now, Jack. Call you later."

She hung up quickly, grabbed her travel bag which was lying on the bed and ran from the room. She turned from the passenger elevator and went to the other end of the hall, found a freight elevator, and pushed the down button. In

205

what seemed like an eternity, the doors opened and Karen stepped in to the empty car. She pushed the basement button and the doors closed and the elevator began its descent. At the basement level, Karen stepped out, and now found herself facing the doors to the laundry. To the left was an exit door. She ran through it, and now was in an alley behind a San Francisco hotel in the chilled night air. I'm getting really sick of this, she said to herself and started running toward the street. But then she stopped, turned around and headed in the other direction to the street on the other side of the hotel. I've had enough of that hotel and anyone who is watching it, she told herself. Amazed that she had got in and out, she started walking. She didn't know where she was going, but she just knew she needed to get as far away from Hotel Sheraton as she could. Reaching a corner, she turned to find herself in front of a theatre. She walked to the box office and inquired after the show.

"It's been playing for over an hour," the attendant told her. "There will be an intermission in five minutes."

"I would like to buy a ticket," Karen said to the fortyish, balding man.

"But it is half over," he said.

"I don't care. I love this play. I just want to see the ending again. I didn't know it was here, or I would have come sooner."

He looked at her oddly, but handed her a ticket. She reached for her wallet, but he said, "No, you go on in. There were empty seats tonight, anyway."

"Thanks," she said, and walked toward the entry doors, trying to hide her suitcase at her side. She entered the lobby, and the clerk went back to his book. He saw all kinds in this city.

Chapter Twenty

When Sarah and Charles entered the suite, Jack immediately approached the President and said, "We need to talk now, sir. About the phone call."

Charles pulled the cell phone from his jacket and said, "Yes, we do. We won't have much time later. Both the mayor and the police commissioner were at the dinner tonight, so I know they will be here soon."

Jack was hesitating, just looking at Charles then at Sarah, unsure of what to say. He certainly could not speak of the planned liaison in front of Sarah.

"What is it, Jack? What do you know?" Charles asked him.

Charles deduced that the room downstairs might have been for him and the woman, but he was not sure, as Jack had never before been privy to his assignations. But this was a bizarre night.
He looked around the suite, seeing Daniel's body in the room to the left. "Jack, let's go into this other bedroom. Sarah, we will only be a minute." They both walked from the living room into a small bedroom and Jack closed the door. Sarah watched them go. She glanced at Daniel's body, and went to sit down on the couch facing the Bay. She laid her head back on the pillows and closed her eyes.

Inside the bedroom, Jack began. "I don't really know where to start, so I am just going to start from the beginning. This morning, actually. Karen Moss approached me in the lobby of the hotel, and we went to the restaurant, where she asked me for my help. She said she needed to speak to you on a personal and private matter, but one that if it were made public, would damage you and the whole country." Charles, watching him, listened intently.

"She wanted me to arrange a meeting with you alone so that she could explain things in person. She felt that you were the only one who could help her."

"Why you, Jack?" Charles asked him. "Why did she come to you?"

"We have a mutual friend, Lotta Hernandez. I dated Lotta a few years ago when she and Karen were at Quantico together."

"This Karen is an agent?"

"Yes. For about three years now."

"This is her phone, then?" Charles handed it to Jack.

"Yes, she must have left in a real hurry to have forgotten it."

"Did she mention a tape to you this morning?"

"She did. She told me it was in a safe place."

"And that's all she told you about it? Nothing of its content?" Charles questioned.

"I think she felt the less I knew, the better. But she was so intense and concerned, and I believed her. Was I wrong? Do you know what is on that tape?"

Not answering this, Charles just said, "Go on with your story from this morning."

Jack continued delicately now. "Karen asked me to set up this meeting with you, on the pretext of a sexual liaison. I know, I mean, look, I'm not judging you. But it's not a secret among some of us. I have heard about other incidents in the past. Obviously, Karen also knew that there had been past incidents with other women."

Charles just frowned at him and shook his head. "Continue."

"I talked to Raul and told him I had a woman I thought would be right for the President. I was just taking a shot here that Raul could set something up. And as it turned out, he did. All the pieces fell into place. The meeting, as you know, I guess you know, was to take place tonight in room 1102. The woman was Karen Moss."

"Holy Jesus," Charles exclaimed. "But the meeting didn't take place."

Jack continued. "There was this incident up here."

"So the room you sent Sarah and me to was her room? She was supposed to be waiting there for me, right?"

"Right. But when Raul went downstairs, the room was empty."

"Jack, it is imperative that I speak to Karen. We have got to find her."

At that instant, Jack's phone rang, and he had the brief conversation with Karen. The President listened intently. Hanging up, Jack said, "That was her. She is really spooked. She hung up."

Suddenly, Sarah's words that Daniel was "taking care of things" crashed into Charles' brain. He had a vision of murder. "Her life is in grave danger," he said to Jack. "We need to save her. But if we have her phone, where was she calling from?"

Jack looked at his phone and pulled up the number. He pressed the button to call back, and in a few seconds, a man answered, "Hotel Sheraton. Can I help you?"

"She was in this hotel," Jack exclaimed. She must have been in the room."

"Maybe she is still there," the President said, feeling though that she wasn't. "Send someone to check. Call security and have them check."

"Right away," Jack answered and turned toward the closed door. Then he stopped and said, "But first, is there anything that you can tell me about this tape? Is that why Daniel is dead?"

Charles hesitated for a moment and sighed deeply, "Jack, as it turned out, you and Karen had a good plan. Too bad it never came to fruition. I, like Karen, cannot tell you anymore about the tape, except that she was deadly correct in her opinion that if this tape sees the light of day, I will be ruined. Help me now like you were helping her. Find her, and the tape."

"I'll do my best," Jack answered, trying to hide the worry in his voice. "What about Sarah?" he asked.

"I'll go to her now. We'll talk to the mayor and the commissioner and figure out what to do. Raul will handle the situation here. You go and find that girl."

As it happens, everybody wants to find that girl. But for the next hour anyway, she is safe in the orchestra section of the Orpheum Theatre. Not that she is really watching the play. She's not. She is desperately thinking how to get out of San Francisco with her life. She secretly wished for Father Bruce to miraculously appear, rather like Christ, and save her. It won't happen, I know, she told herself, but it is comforting to think about it.

Jack did as the President asked. He left to find that girl. Before he left, he briefed Raul on all that he could tell him, essentially, that they were waiting for the San Francisco mayor and police commissioner to sort out the body in the bedroom.

"And the eventual fall out?" Raul asked him.

"You've got a better mind than mine to handle that one," Jack told him, and left for the lobby. He stopped in a corridor facing the front doors, and made a telephone call. He had the number previously in his phone.

Morris Winston answered, and Jack explained that Karen was in San Francisco, somewhere very close to the Sheraton. Morris was also close by, and with him was a person he had interviewed earlier. Perhaps Karen's prayer was about to be answered.

Chapter Twenty-One

As Natalie sailed into the San Francisco night, Serge ran from the roof to the elevator and down and out of the hotel. He walked away briskly from the building, never looking back. He heard the sirens from the fire trucks and ambulance which he guessed were driving to the scene of the young woman sprawled out on the ground, fatally shot, then thrown from the roof of the hotel. It was a scene he didn't like to imagine. He and Natalie had been friends. He, at that moment, questioned his profession. Where had his life taken him? He had gone from the "almost" valedictorian of his high school class to hired assassin. Who was to blame for this? Maybe it was the "almost" that changed his life. The thought of Karen brought him back to the moment.

Now, I must find her, he told himself. But how? This was San Francisco. In any city it would be difficult, nearly impossible, but in this town, anything goes. She could have transformed herself again. He slowed his pace after the sirens quieted and thought about where she might be. She was most likely in the hotel room with Natalie when he called from the lobby. That was only thirty minutes ago. Now he realized why Natalie had chatted with him so long. She was giving Karen a head start. Now Serge knew from his contacts that Karen had an appointment in the Sheraton, set for this evening. Obviously, she had left the hotel, but perhaps she had gone back. Maybe this meeting was still on. He decided to start there. He hailed a cab, and in five minutes, he was standing again outside the doors. The security booth was still in operation, and he pondered what to do with his weapons. If only the person who had so thoughtfully left them outside for him were here now to take and keep them for him again until needed. He dialed Acer and waited for an answer.

"Tell me you have good news," Acer said immediately.

"No, but I'm close. I need you to have someone watch my satchel for me while I am in the hotel. I want to get it again when I come out."

"That's it? What have you found out? Do you have the girl?"

"No, but I'm close."

Acer could tell from Serge's voice that the simple "No" answers were all he was going to get right now from Serge. So he agreed without demanding more information.

"I'll call my man and have him hold them for you. Call me when you want to retrieve them."

He hoped that Serge was as close as he said, and that he could call and tell Daniel that they had succeeded in finding the girl and the tape. If, that is, Daniel would answer his phone. He had been calling for the last 45 minutes, and there was no answer.

Serge entered the hotel, passed through security, and took the elevator to the eleventh floor. The doors opened, and Serge stepped into the corridor. At once he saw at least ten men in suits outside the door to Karen's room. He suddenly wanted to disappear. But he knew he must at least act like he had legitimate business on this floor. So he started down the corridor, smiling slightly. The room door was open, and there were more people inside. He walked past and stopped in front of a door on the other side of the hallway. There he knocked on the door, and said out loud, "Sally, it's me Vince. Are you ready?"

He looked back at the men, and smiled again. Thankfully, no one came to answer his call. He knocked once more, but lighter this time. He waited for a few seconds, then turned and retreated the way he had come. "Guess she already left," he said as he passed by the group of men.

They did not speak, but watched him closely. He did not allow himself to breathe until he was on the elevator and traveling down to the lobby. Even then, he was sure he was found out. He had escaped all those secret service agents, which of course they were, he told himself. And he concluded, the President himself is most definitely involved. Now, he wondered if Karen had been detained by them. He walked into the lobby and stopped to call Acer. "I'm leaving now," he told him. Then he hung up.

A phone rang behind him, and he looked back at an agent taking a short call, then walking to the doors to go outside. He was carrying Serge's satchel. Serge watched him leave, then followed him outside. After the man set the satchel in the assigned spot, Serge approached him and told him in a low voice, "Meet me in the bar across the street. It's time we talked."

Serge then picked up the satchel, crossed the street, and disappeared into the bar. In five minutes, the agent joined him there. Serge and Acer's operative from the Secret Service had a ten minute conversation over a beer, and Serge learned that the President and a large constituency were staying in the hotel. There had been some commotion earlier in the evening when the President had been called away from a dinner for some emergency at the hotel. He didn't know what it was though. All the activity had been going on inside the hotel. Serge asked him if he had seen Karen enter the hotel in the last hour. The man did not know Karen, but when Serge described the good looking, blonde woman, he remembered immediately. Yes, he told Serge, she entered the hotel about ten minutes before Serge arrived. He had not seen her leave. Now Serge was really perplexed. She went into the hotel, but had not gone out? Not by the front door anyway. But, maybe all the agents in the corridor had something to do with her. Maybe now, she was with the President and the secret service. He needed to talk to Acer. Serge told the operative to leave, and in two minutes, he followed him out the front door of the bar. To his surprise, as he stepped onto the street, a black limousine pulled up in front of the hotel, and two men in tuxedos got out and went into the front doors. He recognized one of the men as the mayor of San Francisco, but he didn't recognize the other man. He then went back into the bar and sat at a table where he ordered another beer and called Acer. Acer confided the details he had just learned of the evening. Daniel had been shot. No one knew who did it, or if they did, they were not talking. Daniel and the first lady had been together in the Presidential Suite.

"Was Daniel Slobe paying you to find the tape?"
"Yes," Acer confided. "It was him."

"So, the person who wanted this tape, and Karen Moss, is deader than a door nail?"

"That's right, Shakespeare. The first person who wanted this tape and the girl is now deceased. But now we have another player. I was contacted an hour ago by someone else.

Whatever is on that tape must be earth shattering for the President."

"You have been contacted by the President?" Serge asked.

"Not directly," Acer told him. "But, I can't tell you anymore. All I can say, and I can't emphasize this too much, it is fucking critical that we get this tape. Now what do you know of the girl? We know she is in the city, and the President has instructed the Secret Service to look for her, too. If they find her first, the deal is off with you. But, if you find her and the tape, I am authorized to double the payment."

Serge, after hearing all of this, took a deep breath, considered the situation, and said, "I will find her and the tape. But tell me what is going on in the hotel. The place is swarming with agents on the floor where Karen and I were last together."

"Well, first of all, Daniel Slobe was shot dead, and now the President has instructed everyone to find Karen Moss. Maybe she killed Daniel."

Serge thought this over in his head and knew this was not the case. Maybe this was a ruse by the President to cover up the person who really shot Daniel.

"Acer, do you know of anyone who would want Daniel dead?"

"I don't know why she would want him dead, but he and the first lady had been sleeping together for years."

Suddenly, a light went off in both of their heads, Sarah Hamilton and the chief of staff. One is now dead, and there exists a tape which will be damaging to the presidency if it sees the light of day.

"I wouldn't want to be this Karen right now," Acer said.

"Nor I," said Serge. "I'm going to find her. I'll be in touch," he said, and disconnected the call.

Chapter Twenty-Two

It was the final act of the play, and Karen looked again at her watch. In a few minutes, she would have to leave the theatre, suitcase in hand. She sat up in her chair and glanced around the auditorium. There were exit doors on each side of the stage and one at the front. Each was equipped with an emergency handle, and if activated, an alarm would sound. She assumed these doors would not be open after the play concluded. That meant that the only other way out was to exit the theatre into the side corridors and walk to the front door. She looked back and up toward the balcony. There had to be an exit up there, but it too was probably alarmed. And once out that door, she would no doubt be at the top of an iron staircase which ran down the back of the building. She would need to exit out of the front with the rest of the audience. They would at least make some cover for her.

She knew intuitively that the President was searching for her. Maybe it had been him all along, and not Daniel who had been trailing her. Escaping from Serge was one thing, but escaping from the secret service, the FBI, and God knows who else, was quite another. She had trusted Jack, and he her, but she was sure he had confided everything to the President by now. But how did the President know what was on the tape? Did he know? Karen was sure he did. There was just something in Jack's voice when she had spoken to him. If she could just get to her car, there was a chance she could get out of the city. She had parked it on the street, by a small playground. No doubt it had been ticketed by now. My God, she thought, what if it has been towed away? Why didn't I take Natalie to my car and drive us both away hours ago? But she was too shaken then, and still thought Natalie might kill her. We could be on our way to Mexico, Karen told herself, but it was too late for these kind of recriminations. Hopefully she would see Natalie again, but deep in her gut, she knew it would never happen. She knew she should hate Natalie for what she had become, but they had too much history, and Karen loved her friend.

She pulled her satchel from under her seat and took out an envelope, which she placed in her purse. She also removed a black wool hat which she placed on her head. Then she closed the case and pushed it back under the seat. Thankfully, everyone was engrossed in the final moments of the play, so this action went unnoticed. When the play ended, she would exit with the other patrons and start walking to her car, or Father Bruce's car, as it was.

The curtain came down, and the audience began to clap. The curtain opened, and all the actors appeared on stage holding hands. They walked to the front of the state and the applause continued. Now one, and then another, stepped forward, and soon the audience was up and giving a standing ovation. Karen looked at the man next to her and said, "It was marvelous, wasn't it?"

"Wonderful," he replied. "Just wonderful."

The leading man and woman stepped forward and took a final bow. The applause continued until all the actors stepped back, and the curtain closed. The crowd now began to exit the rows for the side corridors. Karen followed the man she had spoken to and the woman he was with. As they approached the doors, she said to both of them, "I think that is the best performance I have ever seen."

The woman answered, "Yes, it was splendid. Had you seen it before?"

"Yes, in London," Karen lied, but she needed to keep them talking until they were on the street and headed away from the theatre.

"London," the woman replied. "How exciting."

"Yes, my work took me there for a few months last year, and I saw a lot of theatre."

Now, they went through the front doors and were on the street. The couple turned to go in a different direction than Karen, so she said, "Have a nice evening."

"And you also," the woman replied.

Karen navigated to the inside of the sidewalk and was shielded from view by the stream of people leaving the performance. It was ten blocks to the car, and it was dark. Maybe she would make it.

Chapter Twenty-Three

Serge hung up from Acer and continued to sip his beer. He thought about his earlier conversation with Karen. She had driven a car to San Francisco, but had not parked it in the hotel garage. That meant that she had a car near here. She may have already reached her car and driven out of the city by now. Surely it was not her car, but probably a rental or that of a friend. If it was a rental, the secret service would know about it by now. If it belonged to a friend, that was a different matter. He thought again that she might still be in the hotel, but dismissed that idea. She must have been scared by something. But, it she was going to speak to the President, why not just go to him, in the hotel. However, if Acer was involved now with the President, Karen was in grave danger from him. If the President was dealing with Acer, he was ruthless. Serge deduced that she must be hiding somewhere, in another hotel, a restaurant, a bar. She would have to come out sometime. He decided to hire a taxi and just drive the streets in the area and see if he could find anything. Maybe he would get lucky. He had before.

He left the bar and got into a taxi, instructing the driver to slowly cruise the streets as Serge directed him. Willing to oblige, the driver set off combing the streets around the hotel. They had been driving for fifteen minutes and had seen no sign of Karen. Serge thought that maybe Karen had returned to Natalie's hotel. If nothing turned up in this area, he would switch to that area. As they turned a corner, Serge noticed a crowd leaving a theatre. He told the driver to slow down, and he surveyed the crowd. It was dark, but there was some light from the front of the doors and the marquee. He noticed a young woman talking to a man and woman, while pushing her long blonde hair up into a hat. It was her. "Pull up a little and stop," he instructed the driver. The driver did as he was told, and stopped by the side of the curb in front of the theatre. Serge handed him two one hundred bills, and got out of the car. He was now only fifteen feet from Karen.

She drifted to the inside of the sidewalk and mingled with the crowd. Serge did the same. He let her walk ahead of him, but he kept his eye closely on her movements. He could not believe that twice in one night he was lucky enough to find her. This time, he would not let her get away.

As he walked, he felt for the revolver in his pocket. He kept following a few paces behind Karen, and the crowd began to thin. Soon, there were only two people, a man and a woman, between him and Karen. Karen had not looked back. They continued to the end of the second block, and Karen stopped to cross the street to the left. The light was red, and she stopped at the corner. Serge walked quickly to the corner and turned to the right and stopped about ten feet from the corner and waited for the light to change. When it turned green, Karen began to cross the street, and Serge followed. The man and woman had continued straight down the street. Serge could have taken her now, but he wanted her to get to a car if she had one. Then they would be contained together. He slowed his pace and decided to cross to the other side of the street, just in case she felt someone behind her and turned around. Now, he looked across the street and kept pace with her. They reached another intersection, and both waited for the light to cross. Karen crossed the street, but then turned left, and Serge had to run across traffic to keep up with her. He held back, though, and was about to cross over to the other side of the street, when she suddenly crossed the street and began to run. He didn't think she had seen him, so why was she running? He stayed on the other side of the street and walked faster to keep her in view. At the next corner, she bolted across the street and ran into a park. It was fairly well lit, and Serge had only a hope that she wouldn't turn around and see him. He followed her as closely as he could, and she stopped running at the other side of the park and walked through a children's play yard toward a beige sedan. She stopped and reached inside her purse then took out a set of keys and unlocked the door. When she opened the door, he pounced on her and shoved her into the car.

He held on to her arm as he pushed her over the console into the passenger seat. Karen screamed in horror.

"Oh my God! How did you find me?"

"Fate," he answered, and pulled his gun from his pocket and pointed it at her head. "Hand me the keys," he commanded. She did as she was told.

"Where is Natalie?" she asked him.

"Dead."

Karen was silent. All the stress of the last seven days coursed through her body, and she almost collapsed.

"Why did you go back to the hotel?" Serge asked her. "Why didn't you just run? You had a chance then."

"I wish to God I had, but I still thought I could straighten things out."

"You mean with the President, right?"

She looked at him oddly, "Who have you been talking to? What else do you know?"

"I know that the chief of staff has been murdered, shot in the stomach, probably by the first lady. I know that the mayor and the San

228

Francisco police commissioner went into the hotel about half an hour ago. I also know that the President is quite desperate to find you and get this tape."

"You are really something," Karen said, regaining her strength. "Pure evil, and yet so God damned lucky." Karen looked him over, tracing a line in her mind from his dark eyes, and down his chest, to the steely revolver he held in his hand.

"Not lucky, smart. Persistent. Now, let's quit playing games. Tell me where the tape is and take me to it."

Still, she did not speak. All the events of this day were bubbling around in her mind. Meeting Jack, buying red shoes, seeing Natalie, escaping from Serge, running from the hotel, and now, being here in this car which belonged to Father Bruce. A hundred ideas came into Karen's head, lies she could tell, places she could take him to kill time, and it always came back to the same thing. When he had the tape, she was a dead woman.

"All right, Serge," she managed to say. "You are right. It is time to quit playing games. How much money are you getting for me and the tape?"

"Twice as much as it was in the beginning. You are more valuable now."

"And the pockets deeper, right?"

"Very much so. And more deadly."

Karen shivered. "Start the car Serge. I will take you to the tape."

As Serge starts the car, Karen is desperately thinking of ways to stall and save her own life. If she stays in San Francisco, where she is a wanted woman, she stands a chance. Maybe the secret service will find her. She'd rather take her chances with them instead of Serge. But, she realizes that Serge must have connections with the secret service also, or how would he know so much of this nights events. In her mind, she still has not given up on the idea of talking to the President, even if, from what she concluded from Serge, he is the one who has doubled the price on her head.

"Which way?" Serge asked her as he pulled from the parking space, using one hand on the wheel and the other holding the gun on his passenger.

"Just go straight for two blocks, then turn left," she told him, as she pulled off the hat and shook out her hair, letting it flow down onto her shoulders. Serge watched her as she removed the hat. He turned left after two blocks. "Now?" he asked.

"Three blocks up and make another left."

"That's heading back to the hotel. You left the tape in the hotel?"

"That's where I spent most of my day, Serge. In expectations of showing it to the President."

Serge fell easily for this lie, and he wondered as he drove how in hell they would get back into the hotel. "You can't go near that hotel," he told her. "They will pick you up in a heartbeat."

"I didn't say it would be easy. You want the tape. It's in the hotel."

"If you left it in the room, I can guarantee you it is gone now. There were at least ten agents in that room earlier this evening."

"You were there again, too?" she asked him with surprise.

He looked at her and forced a grin. "Great minds?"

"Sick minds. Stupid minds," Karen said without a smile. "It didn't help either one of us."

Now Serge was left to think of a way to get into the hotel with Karen in tow and not be discovered by the mass of security guards. For this he needed Acer's help. Acer's man could get them in and provide some cover somehow. But he could not get to his cell phone, drive the car and keep a gun on Karen all at the same time. He pulled over and stopped the car. He opened his door and looked at Karen and said, "Don't move. I need to make a call." Karen remained still, and watching Serge on his phone, felt a little closer to safety. Serge bought the story of the tape being in the hotel. He didn't realize that in actuality it was hidden out of the country, in Mexico.

"Put you hair up under the hat," Serge instructed her as he got back in the car. "Do you have any dark glasses in your bag?"

"I do," she answered.

"Well, put them on. And leave them on. Remember, I will have a gun on you all the time."

Karen wanted to ask how he would get through security with the gun, but realized that his contact would take care of that. Serge pulled the car into the parking garage of the hotel, bypassing the valet and heading for self-parking. Karen scanned the garage for agents.
Serge pulled the car into a parking place close to the elevator. As he put the car in park, he asked

Karen, "Where do we go from here? And, no tricks. I have people on the inside of this hotel, just waiting for us to come upstairs."

"I put it in the hotel safe," she lied. "I didn't have time to get it out the last two times I left here."

Serge believed her, and keeping the gun pointed at her, opened the car door with his left hand. "Open the door and get out slowly," he commanded her.

He quickly exited the car, and ran to the passenger side and watched as Karen slowly opened the door, got out, and stood up. At this moment, a row over from them in the lot, two men were stepping out of a black sedan. One of the men looked toward the elevator, and recognizing his car, studied the man and woman standing beside it.

"Morris," he exclaimed to the man standing beside him, "it's her by that car. Over there," and he pointed toward his car. "With that man."

Morris looked over at the two people, and Bruce yelled, "Karen!"

Karen looked back, and screamed, "He's got a gun!"

Serge immediately grabbed Karen by the hair and fired a round at Winston and Bruce.

Winston ducked behind a car, and Bruce did the same. Serge pushed the button for the elevator, and then Winston fired a shot that just missed him. Serge fired back and pushed Karen toward the beige car. "Get in," he yelled at her, and shot again at Winston.

Just then, five secret service agents ran down the ramp into the garage, each with guns drawn. Father Bruce stood up and yelled at them, "Don't shoot the girl. Don't shoot!"

Karen did as she was told, hoping that Serge would start the car and stop shooting at Father Bruce. Serge started the car and backed out of the space, shifted into drive, and turned toward the ramp to the street. He gunned the accelerator, and sped out of the garage. The secret service agents fired at the car, and Karen slid down in the seat as the bullets came in through the back window. Neither she nor Serge were hit.

Winston ran to his car, jumped in and started the ignition. Bruce ran after him and jumped in the passenger side.

"You shouldn't come this time. It's too dangerous." Winston shouted at him.

"I'm coming," Bruce said defiantly. "Just stay with them."

Like a directive from heaven, Winston sped out of the garage in fast pursuit of Father Bruce's old brown sedan. Serge and Karen were now about half a block in front of them, and traveling about fifty miles an hour on the busy street. Winston and Bruce followed, dodging in and out of traffic and running through red lights to stay close.

Serge was driving recklessly in and out of the traffic also. Karen suddenly spoke. "I lied before. The tape is not in the hotel. I left it in Mexico, days ago."

Serge looked at her and said, "Why should I believe you now? You've done nothing but lie about this tape from the beginning."

"I'm tired of lying," she answered him. "I just want to get this over with." In reality, she just wanted to get Serge out of San Francisco, to put distance between him and Father Manning, for above all else, she didn't want Bruce to be hurt, and she knew what Serge could do if anyone got in his way.

"We need to go south," she told Serge. "You need to get to the Golden Gate Bridge."

There were signs indicating the Golden Gate Bridge straight ahead, and Serge increased his speed. Now Karen's sense of direction had never been too good, and crossing the Golden Gate Bridge would not take them south, but north. Serge, however, was less informed than she, and he followed her directions. Behind them now were several cars, all black sedans, Winston and Bruce following the closest. There were also now sirens in the distance.

"It's the police," Karen told Serge. "You see all those black cars behind us? That's the secret service. We'll never get out of here."

"We'll get out of here," Serge said with determination. "You'll see. They want you alive. Otherwise, we'd both be dead now."

Karen knew he was right and took a deep breath. They were now in a lane of traffic which led directly onto the Bridge. Other cars around them were pulling over to the side of the road in response to the sirens. Serge barreled on, and in two minutes entered the span of the bridge. There were headlights coming toward them, and the sirens were closer now. Serge suddenly pulled over to the side of the bridge and stopped the car. "Get out," he yelled at her. "Get out and stand by the car."

This time, however, Karen did not obey. "You get out, asshole. I'm not moving."

As she said this, gunshots flew into the front window, barely missing both of them. Serge jumped from the car and started firing at the car which had pulled in front of them. He yelled to all who could hear him, "Hold your fire or I will shoot her, and Hamilton wants her alive!"

Miraculously, the gunfire stopped, as the agents processed what Serge had said.

"Throw down your weapons," one of the agents yelled at Serge. "There is no way you are getting out of here."

"If I don't leave, then she dies," he screamed back. "We are going to drive off of this bridge, or she is a dead woman."

At this time, behind Serge and out of his vision, one of the secret service agents had climbed up onto the structure of the bridge. From his vantage point he took aim at Serge, then fired his gun three times, hitting Serge the first time in the temple. The next two shots angled off the bridge into the ocean below. Serge collapsed by the car. Immediately, the police and the secret service agents converged on the car. Winston and Bruce followed right behind them. Bruce pushed his way to the front and took Karen in his arms as she got out of the car. Karen collapsed into his chest and started crying.

"It's all right now," Bruce said gently. "You're safe." Then he added, looking down, "My car, on the other hand, took some gunshots."

Karen smiled and looked at the windshield and hood riddled with bullet holes. She hugged him again and said, "You know, I wished that you would save me, and here you are. It's a miracle."

"It was Winston," Bruce told her. "He has been looking for you all along. Brian hired him."
Before Karen could reply, Jack O'Shaunessey approached them, and said, "I need to take Karen now. Someone is very anxious to meet with her."

Karen stepped away from Father Manning, and said, "I will call you later. Thank you. You saved my life."

"I didn't save your life. You did that on your own," he answered her.

Bruce watched her as she walked with Jack to the back door of a waiting limousine. The limo turned around and sped away from the scene on the bridge. Bruce took a last look at the brown car, shook his head, and made the sign of the cross, silently thanking God that Karen was safe. Then he found Winston, and together they drove off the bridge, back toward the city.

Chapter Twenty-Four

In the limousine, Jack instructs the driver to take them to the Sheraton Hotel. Karen looks at Jack, and before she can speak, he says, "You are about to get your meeting with the President, like you wanted this morning."

"This morning was a lifetime ago. What happened there tonight? Serge told me that Daniel is dead."

"It's true. He was shot."

"By who?"

"The San Francisco police thought it was you."

"Me? Why?"

"We wanted them to pursue you and arrest you, for your own protection."

"For my protection," Karen asked doubtfully, "or Sarah Hamilton's?"

"I can't say any more about it. There will be an autopsy and official inquiry."

"But, you told the police that I shot Daniel, and now I'm not supposed to be worried about it? Are you feeding me to the dogs?"

"No, Karen. We all know that you are not responsible for Daniel's death. The person who shot Daniel will be treated fairly."

"I don't know the meaning of fairly anymore, Jack. I am so tired of all this running and hiding. Does the President know anything at all about what I am about to tell him?"

"I don't know. I do know that he spent time alone in your hotel room with Sarah before we heard from you."

"They were in my room this evening? Before I went back?"

"Yes. I sent them there. I thought you would still be there."

"That's a long story. The man who just kidnapped me was hired by someone to capture me and to get the tape. He was working for someone in a very high position." She looked at him intently, and added, "Was it the President?"

"I don't know," he answered. "But you can ask him."

The limo arrived at the hotel, and Jack and Karen got out and entered the lobby. They rode the elevator to the Presidential Suite. The small lobby in front of the double doors was filled with agents and San Francisco police. Jack and

Karen walked through them and entered the suite without knocking. Charles Hamilton was sitting on a couch staring out the window. There was no sign of Sarah, and Daniel's body had been removed. Karen could see the blood stain on the floor in the next room. She slowly approached the seated man, and introduced herself.

"Hello, sir. I am Karen Moss."

The President stood up and took her hand, and said, "At last we meet. I wish it could have been sooner."

"I'm sorry about all this," she said. "Really sorry."

"Come, sit down. Tell me what you wanted to tell me earlier. I want to hear it from you. I want to know what you know. Start before you left Washington." He looked up at Jack, and said, "Jack, please wait outside, and tell everyone we do not want to be disturbed."

"Certainly, Mr. President. I'll go now. Call for us when you are ready."

Jack then walked out of the suite. Charles sat back down on the couch and motioned for Karen to do the same. Karen also sat down, turning to face him.

241

"It was a Friday night," she began, and thus she began to tell the story of the last harrowing week. In twenty minutes, she reached the last few hours of this day. She told him that Serge had told her that the person he was working for had doubled the payment for finding her and the tape. Daniel, who had originally hired him, was dead, apparently shot by Sarah. Serge and Karen, both, assumed the new buyer was Charles Hamilton.

"Me?" he exclaimed. "It wasn't me. I don't know who Daniel was dealing with."

"Then who?" she asked. They both looked at each other for a moment, then Charles said, "Sarah. It must have been her. She must have known who Daniel had hired to find you and the tape."

"Where is she now?" Karen asked him. "Am I safe?"

"Sarah has been taken to police headquarters. She will be arraigned in a few hours for the accidental shooting death of Daniel Slobe. She told me all about their affair earlier this evening. But, quite truthfully, I wasn't surprised. Not even about the recording. She has been drinking so heavily these past two years, I am amazed that," and here he hesitated. "I started to say that I am amazed that nothing bad happened. Nothing bad, heh? Embarrassing falls at the White

House, scary moments at State dinners, when I was never sure what she would say or do. But nothing like this. I almost think she planned it, to get back at me." Karen listened and said nothing.

"You've told me so much," Charles continued. "We've been here for 30 minutes. I need two answers now. Where did you hide the tape? And, where is the man, Saul, who gave it to you?"

Karen, still fearing for her safety, had not divulged the location of the tape during their conversation. The only person she had told was Serge, and he was dead. The President, and all his secret service agents, along with the FBI, were very much alive. She hesitated for a moment, then said, "I will take you to the tape, and put it in your hands. But I need someone to come with me."

"Is the tape close by?"

"No. South of here. Below San Diego."

"Mexico?"

"Yes."

He hesitated for a moment, then, he said, "I will have Jack make the arrangements. We will take

Air Force One.   I am assuming the location is near the Pacific Coast."

"Yes, but how did you know?"

"Research.   I learned quite a bit about you in a short time."

"And my person?"

"We'll take whoever you want, but they have to be here quickly.   Now, my second question. Where is Saul?"

"That, sir, I cannot say.   I think he left the country, but I have not heard from him since that Friday night when he was at my apartment.   I know you are wondering if he has a copy of the tape. I don't know. I didn't ask, and he didn't tell. I trust him though. I know he wanted all of this to be quelled, but he was deathly afraid of Daniel."

"And rightly so," Charles acknowledged. "Rightly so." He then stood up and went to the door and opened it, calling for Jack. He then looked back at Karen. "Who is it you want us to reach for you?"

Chapter Twenty-Five

After a four hour flight, Air Force One lands at the Zihuatanejo airport. A large cadre of Mexican police in squad cars watches as the plane lands and taxis to the terminal. They encircle the area and wait as two workers tow the portable stairs to the front exit of the plane. The door opens, and Jack O'Shaunessey steps out into the hot Mexican sun. He descends the stairs, followed by five secret service agents. They wait at the bottom of the stairs as the President comes down. After him, Karen and Father Bruce Manning walk slowly down the stairs. A limousine pulls up, and the President, Karen, and Bruce get into the back seat. Jack opens the front door and sits by the driver. The remaining agents enter a waiting black Suburban and follow the limousine as it drives to the exit of the airport and enters the highway going north toward the town. The Mexican police cars follow behind.

In thirty minutes, they reach the town of Ixtapa, and travel along the beach highway passing many luxurious hotels. Karen instructs the driver to turn left into a driveway right after the Palma Real Hotel. He follows the driveway toward the ocean, and the Suburban and the police cars trail behind. The sign at the entrance says "Public Beach". Separating the public beach from the grounds of the Palma Real is a massive sea cliff. Karen tells the driver to stop at the base of the cliff which is at the southern end of the beach. She gets out of the car, and walks to the base of the cliff. Then she begins to climb up the side of the cliff on a small path. Before she has taken three steps, though, two of the secret service agents block her way. They tell her to wait as the Mexican police pull their cars into a line separating the cliff from the rest of the beach. The police exit their cars and secure the area, moving the beachgoers down to the northern end of the shore line.

After this activity of securing the beach is complete, Karen again starts walking up the rugged pathway leading to the top of the cliff. The two secret service men follow her close behind. She reaches the top and looks out at the Pacific Ocean behind her and the Hotel Palma Real in front of her. The President, against Jack's advice, has followed the three up to the top of the precipice. Jack also followed, and now all of them watch as Karen walks over the edge and descends ten feet down the face of the bluff, stopping on a small ledge.

"Be careful, Karen," Jack yells. "Looks like you are going to fall off."

"I hope not," she answers back. "If I do, you'll have to come down here and retrieve this tape."

"I'm coming down," he says to her.

"No. Stay there. I have my footing. Am sitting down now."

They all watch over the edge as Karen sits on the ledge and reaches back into the rock face with her left hand and pulls out a small plastic Ziploc bag. In the bag is an SD card. She stands up and hands the bag to Jack who has made his way down to the ledge. Karen and Jack climb back up the hillside, taking some assistance from Charles, who has been watching all in silence.

Once secure at the top of the cliff, Jack hands him the tape. "So this is the tape."

"It is, sir," Karen tells him, "I would suggest that you do not view it. Take my word and just destroy it."

"Thank you for your concern," he answers her, then adds, "I'll consider that. Let's get back to the plane now. We can't keep this beach closed any longer."

They descend to the cars, and the entire caravan enters the highway, going south toward the airport. On the way to the airport, they take a detour into the town of Zihuatanejo. The limousine pulls up in front of a small hotel located on the beach. Karen, Bruce, and Jack get out of the car.

Jack gives Karen a hug, and says to her, "This has been quite an experience. I always hoped I would connect again with Lotta, but I never dreamed it would be anything like this. Good luck to you. Do you need anything before we leave?"

"I need a phone."

Jack reaches into his inside pocket and produces a phone. "Here, we got you a new one."

"Thank you." What she didn't say to him as he got back into the car, was what she was thinking, that this phone was totally bugged. She would get a new phone later.

Karen and Bruce embrace, and she says to him, "I owe you a car. Did you return the rental I left with you?"

"We returned it the day you left. But don't worry about the car. I already have a new one."

"I shouldn't wonder. What lovely parishioner gave it to you?"

"A very generous one. And, truthfully, it is a newer model than the one you took."

Karen smiled at him, and said, "I will never worry about you."

"But I might worry about you. Let's keep in touch this time. Do you know what you are going to do now?"

"Honestly, no. I have spoken to Brian, and he is coming down here. I need to see where Alessandro died, and see if I can help his family in any way. And, maybe Brian and I can keep that appointment we had to find a ring."

The back window of the limousine rolls down, and the President looks out at Karen and Bruce. "Keep Jack informed of your whereabouts. I might need to reach you. And, again, thank you for your determination."

"I'd like to say it was nothing, but we all know that is a lie. I will let Jack know when I get back to Washington."

Bruce takes Karen's hand, and says, "God bless you."

"And you also," she says, and kisses him on the cheek. "I will let you know about the wedding. I want you to perform the ceremony."

"Of course. Goodbye now."

Bruce gets into the limousine, and Karen watches as they pull away from the hotel, followed by the black SUV and the three Mexican police cars. She feels a bit afraid at being alone, but at the same time, liberated. She enters the hotel and books a room for a week.

Chapter Twenty-Six

One day later, Karen and Brian walk quickly along a beach in Zijuatanejo. They are following directions to find the shack of Alessandro. At the end of the beach, they find the shack, now empty, except for a few goggles and masks, two sets of fins, and a small boy. He is sitting at the back of the shack as he has done every morning since Alessandro was killed. Seeing them, he gets up to flee, but Karen stops him with an arm, holds him back, and says, "It's okay. We are friends of Alessandro. You did know him, right?" The boys eyes her cautiously and does not reply. Then Karen thinks again and asks the same question in Spanish.

The boy responds in Spanish, "Alessandro was my good friend. We used to have breakfast every morning."

"And you come here every morning?"

"Si. I know he is not coming again, but I like to be here."

"You loved him very much."

"Si."

"Como se llama?" she asked him.

"Cruz."

Karen sees that the boy is looking at a picture taped to the window, and walks closer to look at it. It is a photo of herself, Natalie, and Alessandro, in Monterey, California, near the aquarium. She pulls it down and shows it to the boy.

"See this? That's me. I was a good friend to Alessandro, too, and now I am a good friend to you."

The boy then looks at Brian.

"He is my fiancé," she tells him. "We will be married soon. Right here on this beach."

Cruz still says nothing and continues to stare at Karen.

"Cruz, I am looking for something that I gave to Alessandro. It is a metal box with a jeweled lid of many colors. Did you ever see it?"

Visibly shaken, the boy starts to run out the door, but Brian catches him and holds him back.
"Alessandro gave it to me," he cries, tears streaming down his cheeks. "He said I should keep it in a safe place. He put money in it. For my family."

"Please, please stop crying. It's okay. You can keep the box. I just need to see it. I left something in it that I need now. It is very important. Can you take me to the box? I promise I won't take it from you, or any of the money."

The boy wiped his eyes and looked woefully at Karen and Brian.

"Look, kid, she means it, Brian said to him in English. "Just take us to your house, and let her get something from the box. It is in a special hiding place in the lid. That's all. You can keep the box. Okay?"

Even though Brian said all of this in English, it served to calm the boy, and he shook his head and said, "Okay."

"Let's go," Brian said to Karen and Cruz, and they all three started back down the beach towards the road. There they got a taxi which took them up into the hills to the home of Cruz. Leaving the taxi, they walk into the open air living room of the small shack. The boy leads them to his space, separated from the main living area by a multi-colored blanket hanging from the ceiling. He pulls back the blanket, and they all three enter the space. Cruz reaches under his bed and pulls out the jeweled box.

At the sight of it, Karen gasps. "Oh, my God, it did survive!" Cruz hands it to her and watches her carefully. Brian also watches. Karen holds the box and gently tugs on one of the red stones on the top of the box. It lifts off, and from the small space underneath, she pulls out a small disc, which she puts in her purse. Brian, eyeing the colored stones on the box, asks, "Are those real?"

"No. Are you kidding?"

She hands the box back to Cruz and then takes 500 pesos from her purse and gives them to him also. "Here, take these," she tells him in Spanish. "I would like you to come to our wedding this Sunday at 10:00 am in the morning. You may bring your family if you wish. We will be on the beach near the shack of Alessandro."

Cruz holds the box close to his chest and shakes his head in affirmation, "I will come."

Brian pats the boy on the head, and says, "Good job, amigo. See you on Sunday."

Then he and Karen walk from the house to the street and get into the waiting taxi.

"Well, maybe some of them," Karen says as they depart. Brian looks at her, then smiles in recognition.

"Will he find out?"

"I hope so."

Chapter Twenty-Seven

Sunday morning arrives, 9:45 am, and a Lincoln Town Car pulls up to the end of the road where the beach starts to run to the shack of Alessandro. On the beach is gathered a small group of people, some wearing large hats and sunglasses against the bright sky. A tall man gets out of the car and starts walking to the group. Karen sees him and walks toward him. They meet and embrace.

"Saul," she says, "I didn't know if I would ever see you again."

"Me either. But when you called and left the message with my wife about what had happened, I was so relieved."

"Did you bring it?"

"I did. Do you have yours?"

"I do."

"Are we doing this now or after the wedding?"

"After," Karen said. "I have a boat waiting."

Karen and Brian were then married on the beach by Father Bruce. Cruz, with his mother and three brothers were there as well, along with the families of the bride and groom.

After Father Manning pronounced them man and wife, and Brian kissed his bride, Karen, Brian, and Saul waded out into the ocean into the waiting boat. The skipper helped each of them into the craft, and they started out to the open sea. When they were about one mile from the shore, the captain killed the motor.

Karen and Saul stood together. They each held in their hand a small SD card.

"Ready," Karen asked Saul.

"Ready."

At that, they both threw the discs into the ocean. Then they looked at each other and smiled.

The End.